They made a striking pair, even from a distance. Zac was a good and his short blond cro ng dark ponytail. Even ight for supremacy: Tan e outfit; Zac in his slight ousers with a grey T-shirt and bare arms.

Brock felt a sudden thump of the heart, something that only happened rarely, when he knew he was watching something very special. He stared at Tania and Zac. *Fire and ice*, thought Brock to himself. But which was which?

Look out for more

stories!

Star Crossed
Strictly Friends?
Forget Me Not
Ice Dreams

Coming soon:
Model Behaviour

sweet
he♥rts

Ice Dreams

Jo Cotterill
RED FOX

SWEET HEARTS: ICE DREAMS
A RED FOX BOOK 978 1 849 41216 2

First published in Great Britain by Red Fox Books,
an imprint of Random House Children's Books,
A Random House Group Company

This edition published 2011

1 3 5 7 9 10 8 6 4 2

The Random House Group Limited supports The Forest Stewardship
Council® (FSC®), the leading international forest certification organisation.
All our titles that are printed on Greenpeace approved FSC® certified paper
carry the FSC® logo. Our paper procurement policy can be found at
www.randomhouse.co.uk/environment

Red Fox Books are published by Random House Children's Books,
61–63 Uxbridge Road, London W5 5SA

www.kidsatrandomhouse.co.uk
www.totallyrandombooks.co.uk

Addresses for companies within The Random House Group Limited
can be found at: www.randomhouse.co.uk/offices.htm

THE RANDOM HOUSE GROUP Limited Reg. No. 954009

A CIP catalogue record for this book is available from the British Library.

Printed and bound in Great Britain by
CPI Bookmarque, Croydon, CR0 4TD

*For Georgina Hall,
with thanks for all her
skating help*

Chapter 1

across the ice

The air was chilly, but Tania didn't feel it as she skimmed across the ice, her skates cutting perfect curves in its surface. Wearing a navy practice dress, dark tights and legwarmers and with her dark ponytail, her slim figure stood out strongly against the white expanse. There were other skaters on the ice, but Tania knew that the smattering of spectators only had eyes for her. She could almost catch parts of sentences as she whirled by:

'That's Tania Dunn . . . local skating star . . .'

'. . . doing it all her life, since she was five . . .'

'. . . won the Junior Championships . . .'

'. . . dead cert for the Olympics . . .'

Tania leaned forward into a perfect spiral and there was a collective sigh from the watchers, a mixture of coaches, staff and skaters' parents. 'Such beautiful lines . . .' one of them murmured.

Tania was finding it hard to concentrate, however.

Somehow today she was even more aware of those on the rink side. She shook her head, annoyed with herself. It didn't matter what anyone else said or thought, did it? It only mattered what she, Tania, did, and what her coach said about it. She glanced across the rink, but Brock was deep in conversation with another skater.

Tania took a breath. It was time to try another jump. Every part of her resisted – she knew her jumps were getting worse, not better – but putting things off never improved matters. She stroked her way around the end of the rink and focused on her edges. One moment to prepare . . . then Tania leaped. A vivid image flashed through her mind of her crashing into the ice. She twisted in the air, came down too hard on the outside edge and then fell.

The spectators gasped audibly. Tania, angry with herself, got up immediately and started circling the rink again.

'. . . can't seem to land the double axel any more . . .'

'. . . never used to have a problem . . .'

'. . . maybe not such a dead cert after all . . .'

Tania blinked back tears. She couldn't even hear them properly, but she was sure that's what they were saying. *And they're right*, she thought miserably.

I never used to have a problem with the double axel. I should be working on the triple by now. Why is it all going wrong?

Tania skidded to a stop and tugged on her hair band. Glossy dark hair fell to her shoulders, and Tania scooped it up again and tied it tightly, smoothing back the stray strands. It wasn't any different to how it had been before, but she felt she had to do something to buy herself some time before she tried the jump again.

The air whistled past her as she picked up speed. *It's not that hard*, Tania told herself. *You've done it before, a hundred times. You can do it again.*

She prepared for the jump, taking her time to line it up correctly, then took a deep breath and sprang off the ice. But as soon as her feet left the ground, she knew it wasn't right, and it was impossible to hold position. Instead of a double, it was a single, and not a good one at that.

Brock signalled to her from the side. Tania's heart sank. She knew what he was going to say, but she skated over anyway.

Brock was frowning. 'You're still too tight,' he told her without preamble. 'You tense as you go into the jump. You need to loosen up.'

Tania twisted her hands together. 'I can't help it. It's

3

those people watching me all the time. Whispering when I make a wrong move. They're putting me off.'

Brock glanced over. 'There are always people watching you skate. It never used to bother you.'

'Well, it does now,' snapped Tania. 'Can't you just tell them to go away?'

Brock lifted an eyebrow.

Tania blushed. 'Sorry. That was a stupid thing to say.' She took a deep breath and tried to pull herself together. 'It's fine. I'm fine. I'm just a bit out of sorts today, that's all.'

'You've been out of sorts for too long,' said Brock. 'It's not just today. Those jumps have been giving you trouble for several months.' He squinted at her. 'You look tired, Tania. You're too pale.'

'I'm naturally pale, Brock,' said Tania, re-doing her ponytail again.

'Leave it. Your hair is fine as it is,' said Brock. 'I've coached you for six years now, and you've never been this pale before. You're tired. You've been over-doing it.'

'I'm not tired.'

'Then are you worried about something? School? Friends?' Brock raised his eyebrow again. 'Boyfriend?'

Tania laughed. 'Boyfriend? When do I have time

for a boyfriend, Brock? Or going out with my friends? I don't have any time other than here. I'm always here.'

Brock nodded. 'Maybe that's the problem. You're working too hard. You should have some time away from the ice.'

'Oh, come on, Brock,' said Tania with a laugh that sounded false even to her ears. 'Make up your mind. I'm not working hard enough, or I should have some time off?'

'It's not a joke,' said Brock, suddenly serious. 'You need balance in your life, Tania. It can't all be about the skating.'

Tania shook her head, bewildered. 'But of course it's all about the skating. All my life – it's always the skating. What else is there?'

Brock spread his hands. 'I'm just saying there is such a thing as overwork. You need to pace yourself; otherwise you'll run out of steam. You've always put in one hundred per cent, but recently you seem to be here all the time. It's not the quantity of practice but the quality that counts. It's no good being here all these extra hours if it's not productive.'

'Are you telling me to get a life?' Tania felt frustrated. 'I don't have time, Brock, there's my next NISA test in the spring, and then the Championships. Not to mention . . .' She hesitated, but Brock read her mind.

'They won't even consider you for the Olympic team if you can't land your triple axel.'

'Then stop talking to me and let me practise!' Tania burst out, her voice cracking with the strain. 'I can do it. I just need to do it over and over until it happens by itself.' Turning her back on her coach, she stroked her way to the centre of the rink.

Behind her, Brock looked troubled. He wasn't the only one to have noticed the dark circles under Tania's eyes, he knew. There were mutterings about Tania amongst the rink staff. She had grown up at the rink, putting in hours of practice every week. Even school took second place to her training; if a competition abroad meant she had to miss a week of school, then so be it. Her teachers had given up chasing her for missed homework. Her parents had never needed to be pushy; Tania had enough dedication to sink a battleship.

And it had paid off. Tania was among the top ten junior skaters in the country. She was stubborn; that's why she made a good sportswoman. She would try and try until she made it. And she had natural talent too. Brock had never taught anyone with her combination of talent and determination before. But there was such a thing as burnout, and as Brock watched Tania line up for another double axel, he wondered what had happened to make her so obsessed. He hated to lose any skater, but Tania was his best and now it looked as though she was on a mission to self-destruct.

Tania jumped again, and although she did manage the double, she landed heavily and couldn't keep upright. Her skate slipped from under her, and she fell on her side, most of her weight on her wrist. There was another muffled gasp from the onlookers. Tania bit her lip and blinked hard. Her wrist throbbed, but experience told her it wasn't a bad sprain. She rubbed it with the other hand and twirled it experimentally. It was sore, but nothing more. Probably bruised some ligaments. She slowly got up and brushed ice off her legwarmers.

Brock had made his way round the rink, and now he leaned over the side. 'You all right? Give me a look at the wrist.'

'It's fine,' said Tania. She waved it at him. 'Look. I just bashed it, that's all. Nothing major.'

'I think you've done enough for today,' said Brock.

Tania glanced up at the clock. It showed two minutes to the hour. 'I've got time to get in another double.'

'You haven't. You're too tired. Call it a day, Tania.'

Tania suddenly felt exhausted. Her shoulders sagged. 'I need to keep practising, Brock. How can I get better if I don't practise?'

'You need a rest, Tania. Come on, off the ice.'

'Let me just do a spin,' pleaded Tania. 'I can do spins, you know I can. Just to finish. Let me finish well.'

Brock sighed. 'If you want.'

Tania turned and stroked her way to the far end of the rink, converting smoothly into crossovers, building up speed, and then turning her body into a low spin. Every muscle in her body was aching, but she knew how to control a good spin, and she took it from a teapot up into a layback and then into a blurring finish. The world spun slightly as she ended with her arms in the traditional pose, but Tania had been spinning since she was seven, and it no longer bothered her. Her cheeks were wet, *but it's because I was spinning so fast*, Tania told herself, *not because I'm crying. I never cry*.

The bell rang to signify the end of her session, and Tania looked up to see the next group of skaters already poised at the edge of the rink. She felt a great weariness. Practice was over for another day, but it hadn't gone well. There seemed to be more bad days than good at the moment. *It didn't used to be like this*, she thought miserably. *It's only the last few months. Ever since . . .* But Tania couldn't finish the sentence even in her own head.

She drifted across to Brock and stepped off the ice, the familiar jolt of solid ground beneath her feet. He handed over her skate guards without a word, and she knew he was angry with her for not coming off the ice a minute earlier. Bending down, she slipped the guards onto her blades and turned to take a last look at the rink.

'Hey, watch it!' Tania said crossly as a tall boy bumped her shoulder in his hurry to get to the ice.

He turned; his hazel eyes a strange contrast to the bleached-blond spiky hair. 'Sorry,' he said abruptly, and promptly leaped onto the ice, already travelling far too fast for Tania's approval. She made a disgusted noise.

'He'll never get control of his jumps if he blasts his way through everything. He always takes everything at top speed.'

Brock looked up and grinned. 'Zac's got a lot of oomph all right.'

'Skating takes more than oomph,' said Tania sarcastically. She watched Zac set off around the rink and attempt a double lutz. Exhaustion made her grumpy. 'No warm-ups, nothing. Hasn't he listened to anything you've said? What does he think he's doing?'

'Don't be so sniffy,' said Brock, amused. 'That boy's only been skating two years and he's already achieved more than most people do in ten.'

'But look how far he's travelling in that spin,' said Tania, not listening. 'He must have moved at least two metres. And what has he got on his feet?'

'Nothing wrong with second-hand boots.'

Tania snorted. 'Not if you've got no ambition, there isn't.'

'Ambition isn't everything,' said Brock, glancing back at Zac, who was doing his back crossovers so fast he was overtaking everyone else on the rink. 'Sometimes raw enthusiasm can carry you a long way. And he's talented as well. Just needs polishing up, that's all.' He looked sideways at Tania. 'You could do with some of his rawness. You're *too* polished now. It's made you tight.'

'I am not tight!' said Tania. 'I'm just a bit tired, that's all.'

'Then take a day off tomorrow,' said Brock, his voice suddenly gentle. 'Please. Don't come to the rink. Just go to school and then home to rest. Don't make yourself get up at five-thirty for once. Take a day off.'

Tania's eyes filled at the kindness in his voice. 'I can't,' she said, and wiped her face roughly. 'I just can't.'

Brock shook his head as Tania headed for the changing room. *What am I going to do with her?* he wondered. *My best skater is going to sabotage her own career unless I can stop her. What can I do?* Sighing, he turned back to the rink, and his eyes fell on Zac, who was rashly attempting a triple loop with little success.

A strange idea suddenly occurred to Brock, and a mischievous grin spread over his face. Now that *would* be interesting . . .

Chapter 2

it's all going wrong

'How did it go?' asked Tania's mother Caroline, as her daughter got into the car.

'Fine.' Tania sank gratefully into the seat. She felt so tired.

'Did you manage the double axel?'

Tania's cheeks flamed and she felt hot and cold all at once. *Not now, I can't deal with this now*. 'Can we talk about something else?'

Her mother glanced across at her, a worried expression on her face. For a few minutes there was silence as she drove. Finally, she said quietly, 'Is there anything I can do, love?'

'I'm fine,' said Tania. 'Honestly. Everything's fine.'

'Then why are you biting your nails?' asked Caroline gently. 'You only do that when you're upset.'

Hastily, Tania pulled her finger from her mouth.

'Just habit,' she said. 'I'm a bit tired, that's all.' She stared out of the window again. Almost without realizing she was speaking aloud, she admitted, 'And things aren't going so well.'

'Still? I thought they'd be getting better by now.'

Tania blinked rapidly. *I don't cry.* 'So did I.'

'Do you know why?'

Tania shrugged. 'Everything was fine. But now, all of a sudden, I can't do stuff I should be able to.' *Except it's not all of a sudden, is it? It's ever since ... ever since ...* Tania dragged her mind back to the conversation. What could she say to her mother to reassure her? 'I don't know what's wrong.' *That's a lie.* 'But I'm sure if I just keep practising, it'll get better again. Everyone goes through bad patches, don't they?'

'Of course they do. It's just that you haven't had as many bad patches as some people,' said her mother affectionately. 'It's probably a bit of a shock.'

Tania bit her thumbnail. 'Brock says I've been practising too much.'

'Have you?'

'How can I practise too much?' snapped Tania, exasperated. She drummed her fingers on the car door. 'If things are going wrong, then I need to practise *more*, to get them better again.'

13

'But the practice isn't helping,' said Caroline. 'Is that what Brock says?'

'He told me to get a life.' Tania tried to laugh. 'Can you believe it?' Her eyes clouded. 'As if I've got time for one. Skating is all I do.'

'You don't sound as though you're enjoying it any more,' suggested Caroline. 'You used to love going for practice.'

Tania shrugged impatiently. 'That was when I did it as a hobby. It's my career now. I win competitions. That takes hard work. I can't expect to enjoy it all the time.'

'Even careers can be enjoyable,' said Caroline. 'Do you enjoy *any* of it now?'

Tania opened her mouth to say, of course she did, but the words stuck in her throat.

Her mum said hesitantly, 'Maybe you *should* cut down your practice time . . .'

'Oh, don't you start!' said Tania, the frustration suddenly bursting out of her. 'I can't, don't you get it? There are other girls – Luisa, Zaraah – they're catching me up. I have to stay on top of my game. I can't afford to take time off. I'll lose my ranking.'

Caroline opened her mouth to say, 'Would that be so bad?' but she closed it again. Saying something like that would only make Tania angrier. Caroline never knew what to say these days, but she, like Brock, was worried.

Tania was shaking her head vigorously. 'It's fine. It's just a blip, that's all. I'll keep going till I come out the other side.'

Caroline glanced at her daughter; at the fierce passion in her eyes, ringed by dark circles, and she pressed her lips together to prevent herself replying. She just hoped Brock could do something to stop Tania driving herself into the ground.

♥

That night, after laying her skates out carefully to dry, Tania sat on the floor and did her usual stretching exercises, but her mind wouldn't stay quiet. *You're working too hard . . . You need to get a life . . . You're too tight . . .*

Tania sat in the splits and leaned forward, screwing her eyes shut. *It's all going wrong*, she thought miserably. *It wasn't meant to be like this. I was on top. I was the best. I am the best. But I won't be for much longer if . . .*

A sudden image flashed in front of her eyes. A fall – a crack – a cry of pain.

'Stop it!' Tania said out loud. 'It's not going to

happen!' She pulled herself to a standing position, and her eyes went automatically to the newspaper cuttings over the mantelpiece. TANIA TRIUMPHS! said one, underneath a photograph of a ten-year-old Tania holding a trophy and beaming from ear to ear. TANIA'S DUNN IT AGAIN! shouted a more recent one, as a thirteen-year-old Tania, with waist-length dark hair, posed for the camera in an immaculate spiral.

Tania stared at the photos. Was that really her? She knew it had been; she could remember the days the photos were taken, but it all felt so unreal, almost as if it had happened to someone else. That little girl . . . the one who rushed to get up in the morning so she could be the first at the rink when it opened . . . the one who spent ages looking at the beautiful white boots in the windows and dreaming of sparkly costumes . . . the girl who raced around the rink with a beaming smile on her face just because it was all so wonderful . . . where was she now?

The pictures blurred in front of Tania's face. *I can't cry. I don't cry. Strong people don't cry.* But there was no one watching her now. She didn't have to pretend to herself here. The tears ran down her cheeks and dripped onto the carpet. She couldn't even understand *why* she was crying. Didn't she love skating any more? Wasn't it what she'd always wanted to do? She was doing it, wasn't she – so why was she so unhappy?

It's because it's all going wrong, Tania told herself. Ever since – that accident. And it hadn't even happened to her! But she'd lost her nerve; that ability to throw herself into dangerous jumps had deserted her. Now all she could think about was what might go wrong; how her body might break under the strain of a bad fall.

But top athletes couldn't think like that; not if they wanted to stay at the top. Surely her determination should be enough to see her through this? To fight off the nightmares? She felt angry with herself for allowing one little incident to dominate her thinking on the ice. It was six months ago now. She should be over it! Back on track!

Tania's eyes burned with the hot tears, but she didn't make a sound as she stood staring at nothing. How could she admit she wasn't enjoying skating any more? That she was too scared to jump from the ice in case she crashed into it on her way down? That the reason she kept going back, hour after hour, was because she somehow hoped that her natural ability would magically make everything better again? Brock – her parents – they'd all put so much time and effort (and money!) into her training . . . She owed it to them to be the best. She owed it to herself too, because if she wasn't going to be a professional skater, what was she going to do?

'Who am I if I'm not skating?' Tania whispered to herself, but the question was too hard to answer. Skating was all she'd ever cared about. And now she was almost starting to hate it.

As if from far away, Tania heard the phone ring. There was a murmur as her mum picked up, and then a surprised, 'Brock! Hello. Did you want to speak to Tania?'

Tania held her breath. She couldn't talk to Brock now; she wouldn't know what to say without crying. Hastily, she wiped her eyes, but after a pause her mother started speaking again, in a low tone. Tania couldn't hear the words, but she could guess. Brock was telling Mum how worried he was about her – and Mum would be agreeing. Maybe they'd gang up on her and tell her she couldn't go to the rink any more. Maybe . . .

A wave of tiredness crashed over Tania, and the bed suddenly looked very inviting. Ignoring the quiet murmur from downstairs, she crawled gratefully onto the mattress and pulled the duvet over her head, not even bothering to get undressed.

She'd just have a little rest – a few minutes to close her eyes – then she'd do some more stretching. Just a few minutes . . .

Tania's eyes closed.

♥

'You slept the whole night in your clothes?' Libby said, staring at Tania in disbelief.

Tania yawned. 'I didn't mean to. I just lay down for a bit of a rest.'

'It doesn't seem to have worked,' said Libby critically. 'You still look awful.'

'Thanks a lot.'

Libby grinned. 'You know what I mean. You just look tired all the time at the moment, Tania. And Mr Craven is going to be so mad when he finds out you still haven't finished your geography project. He was mad enough when you had to miss the field trip because of that skating competition.'

Tania shrugged, though inside she felt guilty. 'I can't help it. Skating takes up all my spare time. Homework has to come second. Most of the teachers know that. It's only Mr Craven who gets on my back all the time. Besides, I don't even *like* geography. And what use is it going to be after school? I'm not going to be measuring the water levels in fields then, am I?'

Libby assumed an expression of pretend shock. 'You're not? But I thought that was your ambition, to be the world's greatest water-level measurer?'

Tania gave a rueful laugh. 'Oh, don't, Libby. With the way my skating is going, that might end up being my career after all.'

'Not going so well?' said Libby, looking sympathetic. 'I'm sorry, Tania.'

'It'll be all right,' said Tania. 'I just need more practice, that's all.'

'That's not what you need,' said Libby. 'You need a night out with some mates. Or even a couple of hours. Come into town with me after school.'

'Sorry, Lib, I can't. I have to go to the rink.' Tania re-did her ponytail.

Libby sighed. 'You never go out nowadays. It's months since we went anywhere together.'

'I know. I'm sorry. I have to spend every minute I can at the rink.'

'Are you OK?' Libby peered curiously at her. 'I mean, is anything wrong?'

Tania looked away. 'Why should anything be wrong?'

'I dunno. It's just that recently you've got all serious and . . .' Libby hesitated.

'And what?' Tania glanced up sharply.

Libby shrugged. 'Well – a bit boring, to tell you the truth. Don't get mad at me! I don't mean it like that, you know I don't.' She rushed on. 'It's only that you've gone all serious and withdrawn, like you're living in your own little world. Like skating is the only thing that matters.'

'But it *is* the only thing that matters.'

Libby looked hurt. 'What about me? Tania, we've always been such good friends. You know I haven't minded when you go off to competitions or when you miss my birthday or stuff like that. You've always made it up to me afterwards. But lately . . . ' She flushed. 'I hardly saw you at all over the summer. I mean, do you still *want* to be friends?'

Tania stared at Libby's crumpled face. 'Of course I do! Lib, you're my best friend, you know you are. I don't know what's happening to me at the moment.' Suddenly a wave of sadness washed over her and she gulped. 'Things are going really badly at the rink. I think – I think I might be losing my edge.'

Libby opened her mouth to say, 'Don't be silly,' but when she saw Tania's despairing expression, she put her arms around her instead. 'Hey. You're a brilliant skater. I'm sure you'll figure it out.'

Tania blinked furiously. *What is wrong with me?*

'It's not getting any better,' she mumbled. 'And I'm practising all the time.'

'I get it.' Libby nodded. 'No wonder you're at the rink so much these days. But Tania, maybe you're trying too hard? I mean, it sounds as though you want it so much, you're overdoing it.'

Tania pulled back. *Get a grip*, she told herself. *You're strong, remember?* 'No,' she said more confidently than she felt. 'It'll be all right. I just need to push on through it. The extra practice will pay off.' *I hope*.

Libby patted her arm. 'I'm sure you're right. You've never got it wrong before, have you? I mean, you know what's best for your career. But just remember I'm here too.'

Tania smiled at her. 'I will. And I'm sorry. Maybe I can come out with you soon.'

'That's more like it,' replied Libby comfortably. 'Even championship skaters have a night off, you know.'

Not if they want to remain championship skaters, thought Tania, but she didn't say it aloud. Libby was her best friend and Tania knew life would be lonelier without her.

The bell rang for the next lesson, and the girls got up. Libby grabbed Tania's arm as a tall dark boy walked past. 'Oh my God, it's him. Don't look now – no, I said *don't* look! Tania, do you *want* to embarrass me?'

Tania was amused. 'Lib, if you like Connor Murphy so much, why don't you just ask him out?'

Libby looked as though she was going to faint. '*Ask him out?* Are you crazy? You have *no* idea about boys, Tan. Just you wait till you're totally in love with someone.'

'I don't have time for anything like that,' said Tania. 'I need to concentrate on my skating. I can't get distracted.'

'I love being distracted,' sighed Libby.

♥

When Tania arrived at the rink after school, she was surprised to be met by Brock at the door. 'I thought I told you to have the day off?' He sighed. 'I knew you wouldn't listen. Well, since you're here . . . don't put your skates on. I've got something to show you.'

Mystified, Tania followed Brock through the 'staff only' door and down the narrow corridor to an office at the end. In all the years she'd been skating here, she'd never been into the staff area. 'Is this yours?' she asked, looking around at the piles of paperwork, sticky tape, skate guards and dismantled boots.

'Yeah,' said Brock. 'I don't like to be too tidy.'

'I can see that.'

Brock picked his way to the other side of the desk, where a large pile of brightly coloured posters was slowly edging towards the floor. He grasped one by the corners and held it up. 'What do you think?'

It was a poster for the Winter Ice Spectacular, held every December at the rink. 'It's good,' said Tania, gazing at the colourful images, taken from last year's show and used as a montage. She could even see a tiny image of herself in the short purple dress she had worn for her solo number.

'This year's show should be even bigger than last year's,' said Brock.

'Right,' said Tania, somewhat puzzled. Why was he telling her this? She had assumed she would be doing a number again this year, but Brock didn't need to show her the poster. He could have asked her while they were downstairs.

'I've booked you a slot,' said Brock. 'If you want it.'

Tania smiled. 'That would be great. Thanks, Brock.'

Brock looked hard at her. 'Don't accept too quickly. Think about it. You know things haven't been going so well lately.'

Tania felt her cheeks reddening. 'I know. But they'll get better.'

Brock nodded. 'I'm sure they will. That's why I've given you this slot in the show. A chance to get your teeth into something new. Maybe if you're working towards a performance, it might help to focus you better.'

Tania nodded enthusiastically. 'Definitely. I could even try out something I could use for my NISA test. You know, put together an exam programme as a practice.'

Brock shook his head. 'This is a show, Tania, not a test. I need flashy stuff. Jumps and spins are all very well, but I need a story; a proper crowd-pleaser. More terrific than technical.'

'Oh.' Tania shrugged. 'All right. I suppose that works better in the show.' Inside, she felt a faint flash of relief; she wouldn't be required to show the triple axel any time soon. Maybe a short break from working on it *would* be helpful for her skating.

Brock had put the poster down and was digging around in the pile of paperwork. 'I've got the programme here somewhere. Ah . . .' He scrutinized the sheet. 'Yes, I thought so. I've put you second from last – just before the big finale with everyone on the ice. So I need a really exciting piece from you, something to get the audience up on their feet and cheering – lead us nicely into the big finish.'

Tania grinned. 'No pressure then, Brock?'

He grinned back at her. 'It's good to see you smile again. So you like the idea?'

Tania shrugged, still smiling. 'It's your show, Brock. How can I refuse?'

'Good.' Brock handed her the sheet. 'I'll go and tell Zac then.'

'Huh?' Tania looked down at the programme. Second from the bottom – there was her name, *Tania Dunn* – but it wasn't alone. 'WHAT?'

'Oh, didn't I tell you?' Brock turned in the doorway. 'It's a pairs slot, Tania. You're going to be skating with Zac Maguire.'

Chapter 3

Zac Maguire

'Zac Maguire!' fumed Tania, as she stomped towards the exit. No way was she going to do her normal lesson after Brock's announcement. She was too angry. '*Zac Maguire!*' She was a solo skater, had always been a solo skater. It was her career! How dare Brock make her skate with someone else?

Tania's mother looked alarmed as her daughter got into the car with a face like thunder. 'What happened? I got your message. I wasn't expecting to pick you up for another hour.'

'Brock just told me I have to skate with someone else!' spluttered Tania. 'In the Winter Ice Spectacular. He wants me to do a pairs programme. A *pairs* programme!'

'Ah,' said Caroline, carefully negotiating her way out of the car park. 'This will be with that boy Zac, right?'

Tania turned to her mother. 'You *knew* about this? You knew and you didn't tell me?'

'Brock thinks it will be good for your skating,' said Caroline calmly.

Tania threw up her hands in exasperation. 'How can it be good for my skating? He's a *novice!* I could understand it if Brock had partnered me with someone good, someone who takes it seriously. But Zac Maguire – he's just – just a *beginner*.'

'Isn't Zac the one with the spiky blond hair?' said Caroline. 'He always looks quite good to me.'

'That's because you know nothing about skating,' said Tania sarcastically. Caroline bit back a retort. 'He's only been skating two years,' Tania went on. 'He can't even do a simple spiral properly.'

'I've seen him do jumps,' Caroline interjected. 'Fast, high ones.'

'Yes,' said Tania, 'but he can't land them properly, can he? He just throws himself into them with no kind of preparation. I've seen him do a perfect triple Lutz, but only by accident. The other four times I've seen him do it, he's fallen on his backside – and why? Because he doesn't have any kind of polish, any pride in his tracings. I've never seen him go back and look at the ice after he's finished a spin – and yet he's travelled halfway across the rink! How can he not care about things like that?'

'Maybe he's just having fun?' suggested Caroline.

'Fun!' cried Tania. 'Skating isn't about having fun; it's about getting it right! Pushing yourself to get better and better, not just jumping around and having a laugh. It takes time, effort, precision – what's the point in messing around? Oh, I can't *believe* Brock's doing this to me.' Tania made a furious noise and thumped her hand on the car door. 'It's going to set my training back by *weeks*. The show isn't till December! That's three months away! And I'm meant to be taking my NISA test in January.'

'What did Brock say about that?'

Tania scowled. 'He said I could take it in the spring instead. Like it doesn't matter, like it's just some little test I could do any time!'

'Can't you take it in the spring then?'

'Yes, I *could*, but why put it off?' Tanya bit her nail. 'The other girls are going to overtake me. I need to keep my ranking. This is just impossible.'

Caroline took a breath. 'I think Brock's right. It will do you good to diversify a bit. You're becoming too obsessed.'

'Championship skaters are meant to be obsessed!' cried Tania, incensed. 'How do you think they become championship skaters?'

'You're not just a skater,' said Caroline sharply. 'You're my daughter, and I don't like the fact that

29

skating is overwhelming you. If my little girl is disappearing, then I'm going to do all I can to drag her back.'

Tania opened her mouth to reply, but Caroline went on.

'No, listen to me. I don't like the Tania you've become lately. You're exhausted, you're irritable, you're isolated. You never go out with your friends any more, and you never talk to your father or to me. If Brock thinks this might help, then I'm willing to give it a go, whether you like it or not. And whether you like *him* or not. Zac, that is.'

'He won't like me,' muttered Tania.

'You don't know that for sure,' said Caroline.

'Yes, I do,' said Tania. 'I bet you anything he thinks I'm a Chelsea skater.'

'What's a Chelsea skater when it's at home?'

Tania chewed the top of her middle finger. 'A Chelsea skater is what people like Zac call people like me. A girl who's had everything paid for – skates, costumes, lessons, tests. A girl who's had every advantage when it comes to learning how to skate.'

Caroline laughed. 'Sounds like he's got it right.'

'No, he hasn't got it right,' said Tania. 'What about talent and hard work? Hours and hours of training? You can't get far without those things.'

'Well, it sounds like Zac's got talent all right, otherwise Brock wouldn't have paired him with you.'

'Bet he won't put in the hours though,' said Tania sullenly. She glared out of the window. 'This is going to be a disaster.'

♥

'This is going to be so cool!' Libby danced up and down. 'Skating with a boy, how romantic! It's just like *Dancing on Ice!*'

'Libby, don't be stupid. It won't be romantic. It'll be annoying and boring and I'll have to do all sorts of really simple stuff because he won't be able to do the advanced moves.'

Libby stared. 'I thought you told me he was a daredevil?'

Tania sighed in frustration. 'I did. He is. But he's not *safe*, Lib. I'm not having him throw me around the rink like some sort of soft toy.'

'Wow . . .' breathed Libby. 'Will you be doing lifts and things then? How exciting! Aren't you excited?' She saw her friend's face. 'I guess not. But Tania, isn't this kind of a cool thing? I mean, I know you're annoyed, but won't it be nice to do something a bit different for a while?'

'I don't *want* to do something different,' said Tania. 'I want to be a singles skater. I don't want to skate pairs. If I did, I would have gone down that road a long time ago. And I wouldn't have picked someone like Zac.'

Libby put her head on one side. 'Is he cute?'

'Libby . . .'

'No, really though. Is he cute? Because that makes all the difference.'

Tania shook her head. 'He's all right, I suppose. But Libby, you're completely missing the point. Because of this, I won't be able to take my NISA test.'

'Can't you do it another time?'

Tania gave up. 'It's no use trying to explain it to you. You don't get it.'

Libby wasn't listening. 'Are you practising today? Is it your first session with Zac? I mean – oh, you know what I mean.' She giggled. 'Your first *skating* session with Zac.'

'Yeah,' said Tania. 'Yeah, today, after school. I am *so* not looking forward to it.'

'Do you think I could come and watch?' said Libby eagerly.

Tania turned to her. 'Don't you dare. Besides . . .' she picked up her bag, 'there may not *be* any skating today, not if I get my say.'

Libby stared. 'What do you mean? What are you going to do?'

'Never you mind,' said Tania. 'I think it's about time I stood up to Brock, that's all.'

♥

Brock and Zac were already there when Tania arrived. 'Good,' said Brock briskly. 'Get your boots on and we'll see you on the ice.'

'Hang on,' said Tania, her bag heavy over her shoulder. 'I need to talk to you first.'

Brock glanced over his shoulder at her. 'Can't you talk on the ice? We've got a lot to get through.'

'No,' said Tania, shifting nervously from foot to foot. 'I need to talk to you now. In private.'

Brock frowned. 'Is it about you being paired with Zac?'

Zac looked at Tania and gave her a wave, though his eyes remained wary.

'Look, it's nothing personal,' said Tania.

Zac gave a short laugh. 'Course it isn't.'

Tania turned to Brock. 'Can't we talk somewhere else?'

'No,' said Brock. 'Anything you've got to say, you can say in front of Zac. He's a tough boy, he can take it.'

Zac grinned.

Tania hesitated. 'Well, all right then.' She lifted her chin. 'I don't think Zac is a good enough partner for me.'

Brock raised an eyebrow. 'I think I'm the best judge of that, don't you? I do coach both of you, after all.'

'He's never performed professionally,' said Tania, a pleading note creeping into her voice. 'He's not up to my standard. I'm not trying to be rude about it, but has he actually taken any NISA tests?'

'There's more to skating than tests,' said Zac.

'I know that,' said Tania, 'and I'm sure you're very good. You know, for someone who hasn't been skating long. It's just that I've been doing this all my life.'

'So why aren't you getting any better then?' said Zac, his voice hardening.

Tania felt a jolt of shock. 'What?'

'I've seen you skate,' said Zac. 'You're losing your edge. Those double axels – you used to be able to land them no problem.'

'Leave my double axels out of it,' snapped Tania.

'But they're not the only thing going wrong,' persisted Zac. 'You're not getting enough height on your jumps – you've got scared somehow. I don't know why, because you're an amazing skater, but all of a sudden you're going nowhere.'

'How dare you!' Tania flared. 'You've got no right to criticize my skating! I've been doing it since I was five – you're just an amateur!'

Zac whistled. 'Whoa there, no need for insults. I was just saying what I see, that's all.'

'Well don't,' said Tania. 'You don't know what you're talking about. You can't do half the stuff I can do.'

'Really?' Zac grinned suddenly, and his face was transformed with mischief. 'You want to bet?'

'Oh, come on,' Tania said with a scornful laugh. 'I've seen your skating. You're good, but you're not that good.'

'Prove it,' said Zac. 'Show me what you can do, and then I'll show you what I can do. We'll see who's the amateur then.'

Brock was stifling his chuckles.

Tania was too furious to refuse. 'Right,' she said, stomping off to the changing room. 'You're on. Let's see how you cope with a Biellmann spin.'

Tania's hands were shaking with anger as she tied her laces, but she didn't rush the important task. Zac may not care about the presentation and quality of his boots, but she sure as hell did.

Zac was doing endless back crossovers when she got to the barrier, faster and faster. There were two other skaters on the ice, and he whizzed past them

35

with inches to spare. Tania did some preliminary leg stretches and when Zac spotted her, he skated over, coming to a sharp hockey stop which sprayed ice chips across the mat. Tania was not impressed. 'Do you have to do that?' she asked.

Zac waved an arm towards her. 'Do you have to do *that?*'

'Yes,' said Tania shortly. 'It's called warming up. You might benefit from a few warm-ups too.'

Zac watched Tania as she lowered herself gently into the splits. 'Why would I need to do that? Men don't have to do fancy stuff like that on the ice. It's all about speed and power.'

Tania threw a look of disgust to Brock, who was still looking highly amused. 'You *can't* be serious to pair me with him,' she said.

Brock shrugged. 'Prove him wrong then.'

'Fine.' Tania stood up. 'Move over, newbie.'

'Ladies first.' Zac swept a hand across the rink.

Tania felt more fired up than she had in months. She'd show him! Her Biellmann spins were the talk of the county. No one did them as beautifully and precisely as she did. Spins had always been easy, and Tania had worked on perfecting them so much that she hardly travelled an inch on the ice whilst spinning.

She stroked her way around the rink, building up speed and concentration, and then, as she approached Zac and Brock, she extended one leg behind her and took off into a flying camel spin, the air whistling through her hair. Round and round she spun, gradually reaching behind her with one hand to grab the blade, then pulling up and up behind her head and reaching back with the other hand . . .

Brock and Zac watched as Tania spun for what felt like ages in a beautiful Biellmann spin, hands locked on the skating blade behind her head, back arched in a perfectly balanced shape. Brock nudged Zac and nodded towards Tania's foot, which was revolving on the exact same spot, over and over again, as though it were held there by a metal pin.

Finally, Tania let go of her foot and the spin slowed, finishing with a graceful pose. One of the other skaters clapped in admiration. 'Well?' she said, more than a hint of pride in her voice.

'Very nice,' said Zac.

'Go on then,' said Tania. 'You do it.'

Zac snorted. 'Men don't do Biellmanns. You know that.'

'Evgeni Plushenko does,' retorted Tania.

'Biellmann spins are for girls,' said Zac, but he

looked unsettled. 'You know I can't do that.'

Tania folded her arms. 'So I win, then?'

Zac's eyes narrowed. 'Win?' He paused. 'Fine. If that's what you want. But after I do this, you have to do my move.'

'Fine,' said Tania.

Zac stroked his way round the rink and prepared for a spin. His flying camel was clumsy but he didn't fall, and to begin with the spin was quite respectable. But as he reached behind for his blade, Zac started to lean out of the spin, and his base foot began to move across the ice, tracing a swirly pattern instead of a tight circle.

Tania smirked.

Zac did manage to grab one blade behind him, but he simply didn't have the flexibility in his back to bring the foot up behind his head, and after a moment or two, he let go, finishing the spin with an annoyed expression on his face.

'Lovely,' said Tania sarcastically. 'So graceful.'

'My turn then,' said Zac, looking her straight in the eye. 'You ready?'

Tania shrugged, though inside her heart was racing. What would Zac choose? She crossed her fingers tightly. Let it not be a jump . . . let it not be a triple axel . . .

Zac took off, a steely determination in his face. The laid-back air had gone completely – Zac was serious now, focused on his skating. He raced around the rink, and then, as he approached Tania and Brock, he used a mohawk to get onto his backward inside edge. Tania's stomach plummeted, as Zac lifted his free leg behind him. She knew what kind of jump this was going to be, and she prayed her hardest that he wouldn't land it. If he did . . .

Zac bent, gathered himself – and leaped. Once, twice, three times he spun in the air, and then he crashed down onto his right outside edge. He had spun so high and so fast that the landing was almost disastrous, but somehow Zac managed not to fall. Face flushed with pride, he swung into a hockey stop in front of Tania and said, 'Go on then. Let's see you land a triple salchow!'

Chapter 4

see how it goes

Tania's mouth was dry. Nervously, she licked her lips. She hadn't expected this. A double, yes. Maybe a triple loop . . . 'I didn't know you could do that,' she blurted out.

Zac grinned, delighted he'd impressed her. 'Neither did I,' he said. 'That was the first time.'

Brock let out a snort of laughter, which he quickly muffled.

Tania stared. 'The first time? You mean, you've never done that jump before?'

'Nope,' said Zac. 'I mean, I've done a double before. But I thought I might as well try a triple.'

'You mean, you just . . . *threw* yourself into it and hoped it worked?' Tania couldn't keep the disbelief out of her voice.

'Pretty much.'

Tania shook her head. 'You – you . . . that is just ridiculous!'

Zac shrugged. 'Worked though, didn't it?'

'Bet you couldn't do it a second time,' she challenged.

Zac laughed. 'Oh no, that's not the deal. I only had to do it once. Now it's your turn. Stop putting it off.'

'I'm not,' said Tania, though her stomach felt like lead. Like the axel, the triple salchow had been giving her trouble for months. Even the double wasn't a sure thing any more. She glanced at Brock, but there was no way out from him.

'Your turn,' said Brock. 'Go on. You made Zac do a Biellmann.'

'Yes, but . . .'

'So I win then?' said Zac.

Tania looked at him; his hazel eyes flashed with the challenge. Her jaw tightened. 'No way.' Without a pause, she set off around the rink. Her mind babbled at her: *Use the three turn to get into it, like you've been taught . . . get that inside edge really secure . . . swing the free leg across into the nine o'clock position . . .*

Tania's body tensed up – and with it, her mind, which froze. Panic swept through her like lightning. *A loud crack, a high scream . . .* But she couldn't stop now, and so she swept the leg across, jumped – and knew it wasn't high enough for a triple.

'That was a double,' said Zac mildly.

'I know,' said Tania, irritated. 'I'll go again.' Without waiting for a reply, she set off again. Her hands and feet felt frozen. Tiny prickles of fear travelled up and down her back. She set off into the three turn, but she already knew it wasn't going to work. Images of crashing down onto the ice raced in front of her eyes, the bone cracking and splintering. She took a breath and held it – at the same time knowing this was the wrong thing to do – leaped – felt the free leg wrap too high – knew it was an ugly position – began to come down – reached out with the landing leg – but the ice was at the wrong angle, and the ankle twisted under her . . .

'Tania! Are you all right?' Brock was at her side immediately.

'I'm fine,' Tania snapped, furious with herself and with everyone around her. Her fall had been undignified and painful, and she felt as though she had just been exposed as a terrified fake. How could anyone take her seriously when she couldn't land a jump like that? It was humiliating for a top skater like her! She turned to Zac, panic and adrenalin making her lash out. 'Why did you choose a triple? It's too damn dangerous!'

Zac spread his hands. 'Why did you choose a Biellmann? You know men don't do them.'

'Right,' said Brock loudly. 'That's quite enough from both of you. I think you've proved to each other that you both have skills that the other doesn't have. I believe this is a good pairing. Zac, you can learn precision and grace from Tania – something she has worked hard at over the years. Tania, you've become frightened of jumps and taking risks. Zac can show you how to overcome that. No . . .' He held up his hand as they both began to speak. 'I don't want to hear it. Neither of you can progress much further unless you acknowledge the weaknesses you have and accept help. Whether that help is from me or each other.'

'But my test . . .' pleaded Tania.

'I'm not training you for your test until the spring,' said Brock firmly. 'You're not ready. So it's either skating with Zac or nothing. Your choice.' He put his hands on his hips and looked sternly at Tania.

'That's not fair,' grumbled Tania.

Brock lost his temper. 'I'm your coach and I tell you what's fair. Stop acting like a spoilt child. You're a good skater, Tania, but I've got other good skaters too. They listen to me; they do what I tell them because they know they won't get far if they don't. You've got big-headed, that's the problem. You're a great junior, but you'll never make senior if you don't start dealing with your problems. So put up or shut up. I'm too busy to waste time arguing with you.' He looked at his watch. 'You've got thirty minutes left on the ice, having wasted half of the lesson with your stupid competition. Make good use of it. I've got better things to do.' He turned his back on them and walked off in the direction of his office.

Zac looked hesitantly at Tania. Her eyes were brimming with tears, and she was staring fixedly at the barrier so as not to see Brock's anger. He had never spoken to her like that before. She felt like she was five again and a beginner, not a girl who had won the Juniors and hoped to make the Olympic squad in a year's time.

'Tania?' said Zac quietly. 'You OK?'

Tania blinked and rubbed her gloved hands across her face. 'I'm fine,' she said shakily. 'I'm just a bit – tired, that's all.' She took a couple of breaths to try to calm herself. *Pull yourself together! Why do you have to over-react all the time?*

Zac bit his lip. 'You want to try going round the rink for a bit? Together, I mean. Just crossovers and stuff. Nothing fancy.'

Tania took another breath and glanced up at him. He could have been crowing over her. She had just been taken down a peg, and she might have expected him to be pleased about that. But instead he was looking at her in a sympathetic way, as though he knew how humiliated she was but didn't want to make it worse. Her gaze flicked a moment to the staff door, which had closed behind Brock. Brock didn't do things without a reason, she knew. All these years he'd been her coach, he'd never asked her to do something that would harm her skating. Maybe she should trust him on this?

Tania drew another breath and turned to Zac. 'All right,' she said. 'Just to see how it goes.'

Zac smiled and held out his hand. 'Maybe you can show me how to improve my spins too.'

Tania took his hand, and they moved onto the ice together. 'Maybe. If there's time.'

♥

Brock watched from the little window in the door leading to the staff corridor. He saw Tania reluctantly take Zac's hand and the two of them head off around the rink. He saw Zac suggest back crossovers, and Tania increase the number of strokes to match Zac's. After a couple of circuits, they changed to front crossovers, with a passing step so that every few strokes, one of them passed the other to end up in front. Then Zac came up next to Tania and took the traditional pose of pairs skating, with one hand held in front and the other on her waist.

Brock smiled. They made a striking pair, even from a distance. Zac was a good six inches taller than Tania, and his short blond crop contrasted well with her long dark ponytail. Even their clothing seemed to fight for supremacy: Tania in her usual navy practice outfit; Zac in his slightly too loose tracksuit trousers with a grey T-shirt and bare arms.

Brock felt a sudden thump of the heart, something that only happened rarely, when he knew he was watching something very special. He stared at Tania and Zac. *Fire and ice,* thought Brock to himself. But which was which?

♥

Tania was surprised when the bell rang for the end of the session. The time had flown by and they hadn't even done much.

'That was fun,' said Zac, his cheeks reddened from the exertion. He glanced at Tania to see how she would react, but she smiled back.

'Yeah, I guess it wasn't too bad after all.'

'I'm always up for trying something new.' Zac

grinned. 'And it sounded like a crazy idea at first, but I guess Brock must have his reasons.'

Tania's expression turned serious. 'You know singles skating is my career, don't you? This is only something I'm doing because Brock wants me to.'

'Yeah, I get that. It's just for the show.'

'That's right. But I put in a hundred per cent all the time. In all my training, everything. And if I'm going to skate pairs, then I'll put in the effort. I'll need you to do the same.'

Zac raised his eyebrows. 'Are you telling me to work hard?'

Tania hesitated. 'It probably sounds rude to you. You're not as ambitious as I am. People expect a lot from me. If I'm doing a pairs programme, it's got to be good. Really good. And that means practising every day, sometimes twice a day. I can't work with someone who isn't committed.'

Zac met her gaze levelly. 'I'll match whatever you put in,' he said, and although his voice was low, it had the ring of conviction about it.

Tania nodded, and turned to put her skate guards on.

'One minute,' said Zac. Tania paused. Zac was staring down at her. 'You've got to be committed too,' he said. 'I don't mean putting in the hours, anyone can do that. I know this isn't what you wanted. You think this is going to hold up your career. Well, I don't know anything about that, but I do know I don't want to skate with someone who'd prefer to be off skating on their own. If we're going to work together, you've got to give me a proper chance.'

Tania looked at him for a moment, at the straight nose and the steady eyes, and she nodded. 'Deal.'

Chapter 5

aren't you afraid of anything?

'So,' said Libby, 'how did it go? Did you put your foot down?'

Tania smiled ruefully. 'Yes. And then Brock stamped on it.'

Libby's eyes opened wide. 'No! He really stamped on your foot? With a *skate*? Oh my God!'

Tania laughed. 'You idiot, Lib. Of course he didn't really stamp on my foot. You are so literal.'

'Thank God!' Libby wiped imaginary sweat from her brow. 'For a minute there I was imagining your foot sliced in half.'

'Ew.'

'Well, exactly. So what happened then?' Libby threw her bag onto the floor next to the table and pulled a squashed sandwich out of her pocket. 'Oh no, Mum made me cheese salad again. I told her not to put tomatoes in, they just make everything else soggy.'

49

'You should make your own lunch then,' said Tania primly, producing a small lunchbox.

'You can talk! When have you ever made your own packed lunch?' commented Libby. 'Your mum still makes yours too.'

'Only because I get up so early to go to the rink,' said Tania. 'She says if I made my own lunch in the mornings we'd never get there for six a.m.'

Libby lost interest in Tania's mum. 'Never mind that, what about the training? What about . . .' she lowered her voice, '*Zac?*'

Tania bit into her sandwich and thought back to the previous afternoon. 'It didn't start very well. I was a bit mad, to tell you the truth. Maybe I went a bit over the top.'

'You? Never,' said Libby loyally, and then ruined the effect by snorting with laughter. 'I can't think of a single time you've ever gone over the top before . . . oh wait, except that time you found out Mrs Lafayette had timetabled your French Oral at the same time as your last NISA test . . . and then the time your skates weren't ready when they said they would be and you just went mad because you wanted to practise that evening . . . and then there were the other fifty-three times . . .'

'*Anyway,*' went on Tania, ignoring Libby's malicious

giggle, 'we only did a bit of practice but it was all right. Not amazing, but not as bad as I thought it was going to be.' She hesitated. 'Do I really go over the top that much?'

'Yes,' said Libby affectionately, 'but I still like you. Can't think why.'

Tania pulled a face. 'I can't think why either.'

Libby laughed. 'Oh, Tania! You are so serious sometimes! Maybe that's why we make such good friends. You're too serious and I'm not serious enough!'

'We are complete opposites, aren't we?' asked Tania with a rueful smile.

'Just as well too,' said Libby, picking slices of tomato out of her sandwich and piling them on the table. 'I couldn't be friends with someone exactly like me. I mean, what would we talk about? Except boys, of course.'

Tania watched her friend make a pile of soggy tomatoes. 'That's disgusting, Lib.'

'Speaking of *boys*,' went on Libby, 'what's he like? Zac.'

'He's all right. Not as rude as I thought.'

'Aha!' Libby waggled her eyebrows. 'I knew it! Romance blossoms on the ice.'

Tania shook her head in amusement. 'You have

such a one-track mind. It's not like that at all. He's not even my type. He's far too laid-back for me. I'm really driven; ambitious. He's not like that at all.'

'Uh-huh.'

'What's that supposed to mean?'

'What colour are his eyes?' asked Libby.

'Hazel,' said Tania automatically.

'HA!'

'What?'

Libby leaned forward and waved a slice of tomato at her friend. 'You've noticed his eyes! That can mean only one thing . . .'

'They're either side of his nose?' suggested Tania.

'You fancy him!' announced Libby dramatically.

'I do not!' said Tania. 'Lib, honestly, it's just skating. It's only for a couple of months; just till the show. That's all.'

'Hmm,' said Libby. 'That's what *you* say.'

Tania laughed. 'Even if I did feel like that, Zac wouldn't look at me twice. We're from different worlds. Besides, he knows singles is my career. He's just in it for the fun. He's so laid-back, he'll probably forget all about practice today anyway.'

Libby made a face. 'Say what you like,' she said loftily, the effect slightly spoilt by the dab of mayonnaise on her nose. 'This is the beginning of a beautiful relationship. I just know it.'

♥

As Tania got out of the car for the afternoon practice, she suddenly remembered what she'd said earlier to Libby. Would Zac have forgotten about practice today? Would he have changed his mind? As she waved to Michael on the ticket desk and pushed open the big double doors, she felt momentarily flustered. If Zac had decided not to come . . . how would she feel about that? Would she be pleased? Or would she . . .

Tania drew in a sharp breath. Not only was Zac here, but he was already on the ice. She could tell it was him by the short blond hair and the battered boots. He was in a sit spin, and she watched for a moment as he spun round and round, trying to get into as tight a position as possible. Coming out of the spin, he stopped for a moment, as though dazed, and ran his fingers through his hair so that the little spikes stuck out at all angles. Then, to Tania's amazement, Zac skated back to the patch of ice where he had started spinning and gazed intently downwards. *He's looking at his tracings*, Tania thought with some shock. She'd never seen him do that before.

As if alerted by some sixth sense, Zac suddenly looked up. Tania felt her cheeks redden at being caught watching, but Zac waved cheerfully at her. 'Only travelled three feet this time!' he yelled up, oblivious to the other people on and around the rink. 'Better than yesterday!'

Tania felt her mouth creep up into a grin. Zac obviously didn't bear her any ill will after her outburst. Others were looking curiously at her, but she was too embarrassed to yell back, so instead she went quickly down the stairs to the changing rooms. Ten minutes later and she was suitably attired for the rink, though she still had some stretching to do.

Zac joined her rink side, as Tania bent forward over her knee. 'Thought you might not come,' he said with a grin.

'I thought you might not either,' retorted Tania.

Zac tilted his head on one side. 'I did think about it,' he said. 'I wasn't sure I liked the idea of working with a Chelsea skater.'

'Oh, I *knew* you'd say that at some point!' exclaimed Tania. 'I am *not* a Chelsea skater!'

Zac laughed. 'Boy, you're easy to wind up. Do you have to take everything so seriously?'

Before Tania could answer, Zac had leaped onto the

ice – backwards. 'Hey,' he called. 'I've been working on this step sequence, what do you think?'

Tania placed her right foot on the barrier and stretched out as she watched Zac perform a complicated sequence that looked like a cross between salsa dancing and jumping over hot coals. Unfortunately, he tripped over his own toe-pick as he reached the end of the rink, and crashed into the barrier, narrowly avoiding another skater, who glared at him. Tania stifled a snort.

'I'm all right!' Zac yelled. 'It wasn't meant to be quite like that.'

'I should think not,' came Brock's voice from Tania's left. She blushed, unsure how he would be with her after yesterday.

'Hi, Brock.'

'Hi, Tania. You ready for some hard work?'

Tania slipped off her guards and stood up straight. 'Always.'

'Good.' Brock nodded at her and gave her a brief smile. 'Then let's get started.'

Brock made Tania and Zac skate in straight lines from one end of the rink to the other, trying to match their skating strokes. 'Left . . . right . . . left . . . right,' he called. 'Stop. Now do it coming back the other way, but without me counting. And don't look at each other!'

It was extremely difficult. Not only did Tania have to watch Zac out of the corner of her eye, but she also had to make sure she wasn't about to bump into any of the other four skaters on the ice. 'You've got to be able to sense what the other person is doing,' said Brock. 'You have to know where they are, which edge they're on, without looking. And you have to know their dimensions too. It's like getting a new car. You have to learn the width, how the brakes handle, the speed of acceleration. You have to adapt your driving style to the new car.'

Zac glanced at Tania. 'I think Tania is a later model than I am,' he said. 'And has better road handling.'

'But you have sharper brakes,' grinned Tania, remembering Zac's abrupt hockey stops.

'Enough,' said Brock. 'Do it again.'

After they had been up and down the rink countless times, Brock allowed the two of them to skate round hand in hand a few times. 'You're not trying to do what the other person does,' he said. 'You're trying to find the common ground – the halfway between the two of you. Better.'

Slowly, Tania found she was becoming more aware of Zac's skating style. It was different to hers – longer strides because of his longer legs, and a tendency to lean forward to increase speed – but she had to admit there *was* something rather exciting about trying to skate with him, almost as though they were one person with two sets of skates.

There were only a few people around today, mostly parents and rink staff, but Tania could see most of them were watching curiously, and she suddenly wondered how she and Zac looked as a pair. Were the spectators secretly amused by this strange partnership? Did they see it as a step down for her, the girl who'd always skated solo? *You shouldn't care what they think*, she told herself sternly. *You're not doing it for them.*

'Good,' said Brock. 'And now close your eyes, Tania.'

Tania blinked. 'What?'

'Close your eyes,' ordered Brock. 'Zac will navigate you around the rink.'

Tania shot a quick look at Zac. He looked surprised, but as he caught her eye, he smiled reassuringly. 'Hey, no problem. I've got a good sense of direction. Never driven a Porsche, obviously, but . . .'

Tania laughed nervously and closed her eyes. Her hand tightened in Zac's, and gradually he began to lead her across the ice.

'Keep them closed!' called Brock from the side. 'No peeking!'

Tania felt very unnerved. 'I don't like this,' she

muttered to Zac as he tugged on her hand. 'It's weird.'

'You're doing fine,' came Zac's voice. 'Besides, you've been around this rink a thousand times before, haven't you? I bet you could do it yourself with your eyes shut.'

'That's different,' said Tania, and wobbled slightly. She set her jaw. 'I would still be in control.'

'Relax!' shouted Brock.

Tania heard Zac laugh. 'I don't think ordering her to relax is going to work,' he called back.

Tania felt annoyed. 'I can relax,' she said shortly. Staring fiercely into the blackness, she imagined the ice melting into a huge hole in front of her. And one more step and she'd be falling into it . . . falling . . .

'Um, that's not relaxing,' said Zac. 'Your grip just got tighter.'

Tania opened her eyes and drew to a stop. 'I'm sorry. I'm not sure I can do this.'

'It's OK,' said Zac. 'It'll take time.'

'You haven't got time,' said Brock as they skated over to him. 'You've got three months. To learn how to skate together, get a programme together and polish it to performance standard. So do it again, only Zac, you close your eyes this time.'

Zac grinned, obediently closed his eyes and held

out his hands. Tania gently led him around the rink and was astonished to find Zac simply followed her. Even when she led him into the barrier by mistake.

'Oof!' said Zac as he folded over the top of the barrier, the wind knocked out of him.

'Oh my God!' cried Tania. 'I'm so sorry! Are you all right? I just didn't . . . I mean . . .'

'I'm fine,' said Zac, breathing heavily. He grinned at her again. 'So *you* haven't got much of a sense of direction then.'

Tania flushed. 'I just left it too late to turn.'

'I know,' said Zac. 'I was pulling your leg.'

'Are you really OK?'

Zac patted his stomach. 'Solid as a rock, these muscles are,' he said, and spoiled the effect by wincing.

Tania felt her mouth twitch. 'Yeah, looks like it.' *How can he take it all so calmly?* she wondered.

'What is this, a date?' yelled Brock. 'Get on with the skating!'

Zac straightened up. 'Ready to go again?' he said, and held out his hand.

'You'll still let me lead you?' said Tania in astonishment. 'But I just crashed you into the barrier!'

Zac shrugged. 'I'm sure you'll try not to this time.'

Tania took his hand, and Zac closed his eyes. As she led him around the rink, Tania marvelled on Zac's lack of fear. He'd just had a nasty crash. She wouldn't have blamed him if he'd said he'd had enough. After all, it was her fault – she wouldn't have been surprised if he'd been angry with her. But instead, he just dusted himself off and said, 'Let's go again.' Didn't he mind having accidents and falls? Didn't they make him nervous?

As they stepped off the ice at the end of the session, Tania plucked up the courage to ask. 'Um . . .' she said. 'Look, I don't know how to say this, but – aren't you afraid of hurting yourself, out there on the ice?'

Zac looked surprised. 'Hurting myself?' he repeated, a puzzled frown between his brows. 'No, I don't think I am. What's the point in worrying about something like that? If I thought I might hurt myself, I'd never cross the road, or go down stairs, let alone try a triple salchow. Why?'

Tania shook her head hastily. 'Oh, no reason.'

Zac threw her a curious glance, but Tania was putting on her skate guards and heading to the lockers. He shrugged and sat down to unlace his boots where he was.

Brock joined him on the bench. 'It's about time you got some decent boots, Zac,' he said, 'especially if you're going to be practising more often. Those ones are starting to break down.'

'Nah,' said Zac. 'They'll last a bit longer. Besides, I'm fond of the old things.' He ran a finger along one blade to remove the chips of ice. 'I'll sharpen them though. They're not cornering as well as they used to.'

'You should get a professional to do that,' said Brock. 'They'll do a better job than you can.'

Zac pretended to look offended. 'What are you saying about my sharpening skills?'

'I'm saying they're not good enough if you want to partner Tania,' said Brock. 'Get it sorted, Zac. And get some new boots. Otherwise you'll never keep up with her.' He patted Zac on the back and stood up. 'Good work today.'

'Thanks,' said Zac. He unlaced his second boot and looked up. Brock had disappeared into the staff corridor. Zac's usually cheerful face looked worried.

Chapter 6

haven't you done enough?

'You're on the wrong edge,' Tania observed. 'That's why you're not taking off cleanly.'

'I'm on my inside edge,' said Zac.

'No, you're not. Look, this is what you did.' She demonstrated. 'See? At the last minute you cheated it.'

Zac shook his head. 'No, this is what I did.' He repeated the jump.

'Exactly!' said Tania. 'You did it again!'

'I don't know what you're talking about.' Zac appealed to Brock. 'I wasn't on my outside edge, was I?'

'Yes you were,' said Brock bluntly. 'Tania's right.'

Zac bit his lip and looked at the ice. 'Well, I didn't mean to.'

'It's your boots,' Tania pointed out. 'They're too old to support your ankles properly.'

'There's nothing wrong with my boots,' said Zac sharply. 'They're fine. If I took off from the wrong edge, that's my fault.'

'So do it again from the inside edge,' said Tania, her hands on her hips.

Zac did the jump again, but although it was the correct edge this time, it was clumsily done.

Tania felt frustrated. Zac was such a weird mixture; obviously talented but without the solid training that she had had. He wanted to run before he could walk. He loved jumps and trying out new things, but he still wasn't interested enough in polishing the things he considered boring, like basic crossovers.

They had been skating together for a week now, and Zac's lack of technique was bothering her more and more. She wanted to give him a real chance. Brock thought this could work, but Tania was starting to think that her initial fears about Zac's lack of experience were being proved right. When they skated hand-in-hand or in the traditional partner position, Tania could hear Zac's blades scrape the ice noisily. She had always taken pride in the silence of her skating, and the sound grated on her.

She bit her lip. She didn't want Brock to be angry with her, but she had to say what was on her mind. 'Brock,' she said quietly as Zac practised the take-off position for the jump, 'are you really sure about this? He's not going to be ready at this rate.'

'He's only had a week,' said Brock, watching Zac try the jump again. 'Give him a chance. You didn't get that good in a week.'

'No,' said Tania, 'I got good in several years. We only have three months – less, now. I know what you're trying to do, and I get it, I really do. You want me to take more risks. But I don't think this is helping me overcome that. And he's not going to be up to my standard by the time we get to the show. Wouldn't it be better just to give me a solo programme?'

Brock looked at her. 'I thought you were fully committed to this, Tania?'

'I am!' Tania said indignantly. 'I trust your judgement, Brock.'

'Then keep on trusting. It'll be all right.'

Tania sighed, her eyes back on Zac. 'I'll try. I just get this horrible feeling it's all going to go wrong.'

Brock turned to look her full in the face. 'More wrong than it already is for you?'

Tania gulped and looked down.

Brock paused for a moment, and then called to Zac. 'All right, that's enough. Come off the ice now.'

'We've got half an hour left,' said Zac, his cheeks flushed.

'I know,' said Brock. 'I want you both back here in five minutes to do some off-ice work, OK?'

'You could be more helpful,' said Zac, as they headed to the lockers.

Tania turned, her eyebrows climbing into her hair. 'More *what*?'

'Helpful.' Zac pulled his bag out of the locker roughly. 'Instead of just criticizing me all the time. Saying I'm not good enough. I can guess that's what you were saying to Brock.'

Tania's cheeks flamed. 'I wasn't,' she mumbled.

'You were.'

'Well,' said Tania, embarrassment making her snap, 'it's not *my* fault you keep getting it wrong, is it?'

'I'm doing my best,' said Zac, teeth gritted as he unlaced his boots.

Tania was about to retort when she caught sight of Zac's feet. They were covered in plasters, and there was a strap on his left ankle. Her breath caught in her throat. Zac's boots must be giving him blisters – why hadn't he said anything? And that strap looked serious. When had he twisted his ankle?

Tania unlaced her white boots. Her own feet weren't without bruises and injuries either, but nothing compared with Zac's. She wondered why on earth he didn't simply buy a new pair – get them fitted properly.

If he could afford lessons with Brock, he could surely afford new skates.

Brock was waiting for them when they came out, and led them through a side door into a small dance studio. 'Sorry it's not a bit warmer,' he said. 'We won't be too long.'

'What are we doing in here?' asked Tania. She had only ever used this room for warm-ups before sessions or competitions.

'Lifts,' said Brock.

'Pardon?' said Tania.

'Excellent!' said Zac.

'You can't have a pairs programme without lifts,' said Brock.

Tania panicked. 'What, *now*? We've only been skating together a week!'

'It's never too early to start practising the lifts,' Brock told her. 'We'll start with something really simple.' He made Tania stand opposite Zac and instructed her to put her hands on his shoulders. 'Now, Zac, you put your hands on Tania's waist.'

Tania felt a blush creeping across her face. Skating side by side with Zac was one thing, but facing him in such an intimate position was something else. Through her inner anxiety about being lifted, she was intensely aware of his strong hands circling her waist.

'Good grief, you're thin,' said Zac. 'Don't you eat anything?'

'Don't complain,' said Brock before Tania could reply. 'Thin means light, and the lighter the better when it comes to lifts.'

'Oh, I wasn't complaining,' said Zac. His hands tightened. 'It's just there's nothing of her!'

'I am here, you know,' said Tania. Zac grinned at her. She glared back.

'OK,' said Brock. 'Now, Tania, you bend and push up. Zac you lift her off the ground, just for a moment.'

Tania felt flustered, but there was no option. She bent at the knees, and sprang upwards. Instantly, Zac lifted her up, and for a moment she was almost as high as the ceiling. It was an extraordinary feeling. And underneath her, Zac felt as solid as a rock. *Maybe . . . maybe I won't fall if he's holding me.*

'Good,' said Brock. 'Again.'

After that first lift, he made them try it in different positions – Tania facing away from Zac, then with one leg bent.

'You're strong,' said Brock appreciatively. 'That's good.'

Tania said nothing. The initial fear had subsided, but now something else was preying on her mind. She was acutely aware of the muscles hidden under

Zac's sweatshirt. Up to now, it hadn't even occurred to her to wonder what his body was like under his clothes.

'You all right?' asked Zac, peering at her. 'You look kind of hot.'

'I'm fine.' Tania said, embarrassed. Oh God, he had seen her staring at his chest! 'Let's do that one again.'

'Try a fish dive next,' said Brock.

'A what?' asked Zac, but Tania was familiar with fish dives.

'They do them in ballet,' she told him. 'And often to finish the end of a pairs programme.'

Brock showed Zac where to put his arms and how to lift her. Then Tania took up the position, front leg bent so that the pointed toe touched the knee of the back leg, which was straight out behind her. Zac swung her down in front, so that she was suspended just above the floor.

'Nice,' said Brock. 'But watch your posture, Zac. You look more like a rugby player than a dancer.'

'That's because I *am* a rugby player,' said Zac.

'You need a bit more grace. Be aware of how it looks from the front.'

'My arms ache,' said Zac.

'I thought you said I weighed nothing,' said Tania, her arms still stretched out gracefully.

68

'Yeah, well, you're getting heavier.' He lifted her and set her back on her feet.

'Good work,' said Brock. 'Tomorrow we'll try some on the ice.'

The familiar panic rushed through Tania like a wave. Lifts on the ice! She wasn't ready! What if she fell? Wasn't it an accident waiting to happen? Head down, she barely heard Zac as he called out a cheerful goodbye.

♥

'Was it dreamy?' asked Libby, her eyes unfocused.

'Was what dreamy?' asked Tania, searching through her bag. 'I'm sure I brought my protractor. It must be at the bottom.'

'Being lifted by Zac,' said Libby. 'Was it amazing?'

Tania laughed. 'You have no idea, Libby. Firstly, being lifted isn't effortless. It can be quite uncomfortable. I mean, when Zac had his hand *here*' – she pointed to her left side – 'he was gripping really tight. I didn't notice at the time, but afterwards it really ached.'

'Was it embarrassing?' said Libby. 'When Brock told him to put his hands round your waist. Did you go red?'

Fortunately, Tania was saved from answering by the

maths teacher, who told them in no uncertain terms to keep quiet and get on with the task set. But Libby wasn't going to let her off that easily. Two minutes later, a note was pushed under Tania's nose. Libby had written: *So do you fancy him then?*

Tania felt a jolt. *Fancy* Zac? Of course she didn't fancy him! Frowning, she wrote the word *NO* and pressed so hard with her pencil that the lead snapped.

Libby watched her write and looked up at her friend. Her expression said very clearly, 'I don't believe you!'

Tania bent to her maths again, feeling cross. Libby was so single-minded! Boys were the only thing she thought about! It was inconceivable to Libby that Tania could be skating with a boy partner and *not* fancy him. *Honestly*, thought Tania to herself, *if she could be in my position, she'd know I'm only doing this because Brock thinks it's a good idea. It doesn't matter at all what Zac is like as a person – it's only his skating I'm interested in.*

The fact that he has quite muscled arms . . . and a lot of strength . . . and makes sure he's lifting me as carefully as he can . . . and the way that he looks at me with those eyes . . .

That's got nothing to do with anything!

♥

'Right,' said Brock. 'Just something simple to start with.'

Zac reached for Tania's hand. At the sudden contact, she jumped slightly. 'You all right?'

Tania, furious with herself for reacting, nodded. 'Fine. I'm fine.' *Stop thinking about what Libby said! You do NOT fancy Zac!*

The two of them set off round the ice. At the agreed moment, Tania went into a spiral. Zac put one hand round her waist and the other under her raised leg, and he lifted her a few inches from the ice. Tania felt her whole body tense. Any confusion about her feelings was swept away by the usual chilling fear. It wasn't anything to do with being lifted by Zac but simply the fact that both her feet were off the ice. She was completely at the mercy of her partner. *Must not think about falling!*

'That was good,' said Brock when Zac put her down again, 'but Tania, you've got to look like you're enjoying it. You looked like you'd just swallowed a lemon.'

'I feel uncomfortable,' said Tania, adjusting her leggings.

'You will to start with,' said Brock. 'But more practice will help.' He made them do the same lift over and over again, until even Tania started to relax a bit. *He's not going to drop you*, she told herself. *You need to trust him, remember?*

'You're much easier to lift now,' said Zac in surprise. 'What are you doing differently?'

Tania shrugged, but she felt pleased that he'd noticed a change. 'Nothing special,' she said. *Just stay focused. It's going to be all right.*

'OK,' said Brock. 'Now do the same carry again, but this time, Zac, you do a three turn whilst you're holding Tania.'

Tania's eyes widened. 'You want him to change direction while I'm off the ice?' *But that's a lot more difficult! What if he catches an edge?*

'Yes,' said Brock, holding her gaze.

'OK,' said Zac. He held out his hand to Tania. 'Let's give it a go.'

Reluctantly she took his hand, but the traitorous voice in her head kept telling her this was a bad idea. *He's not ready. You're not ready. You've only just got used to the forward carry; it's too soon.* Tania felt helpless. She couldn't back out of it. She had promised Brock to be committed – she'd promised Zac too. She would have to go through with it, even though her legs felt as though they were welded to the ice.

They approached the agreed point and Tania raised her leg in preparation, taking a shallow breath. Zac lifted her easily off the ice, and Tania felt him tense under her as he went into the three turn. The arm around her waist tightened in reflex, and then he caught his toe-pick, and for a moment Tania felt suspended between safety and disaster. *It's going to happen again! The accident . . . the broken bones . . . and there's nothing you can do to stop it!* Then the world speeded up again as they crashed to the ice, Zac's weight falling heavily on Tania's outstretched leg. She cried out.

Zac was up and off her leg like lightning. 'I'm so sorry, Tania. Are you all right?'

Brock too had rushed over. Tania curled her leg under her, trying to blink back tears. Her leg was strong but there was a lot of Zac to land on it, and her thigh throbbed. Confused feelings rushed through her – relief that there had been no echoing snap of the bone, anger that Brock had let this happen, and shock from the sudden pain. Briefly she wondered if she was going to be sick.

'Give me your hand,' said Zac. He reached down to help pull her up.

Tania jerked back. 'Get off me! I don't need your

help!' She struggled shakily to her feet, wincing as she put her left foot down. Zac offered his hand again as she wobbled, but she batted him away, pain making her unreasonable. 'I said, get off me! Haven't you done enough?'

Zac looked shocked. 'I am really sorry, Tania.'

Brock helped Tania off the ice, his face concerned. 'How does it feel?'

'Painful,' she said sharply. 'How do you think?'

'Can you move it? How bad is it?'

'I haven't broken it, if that's what you're thinking,' she snarled. 'It just really hurts.'

'We should probably get it X-rayed anyway,' Brock told her. 'Just in case.'

'It's not broken. I know it isn't. I can tell the difference. Look.' Tania prodded her leg, wincing at the bruised feeling but knowing everything was where it should be.

Brock looked at her searchingly. 'All right. I'll get an ice pack for the bruising. You sit down.' He headed for the first-aid cupboard.

Zac hovered at the edge of the rink. 'I am so sorry,' he said again, and his face was white. 'Maybe it was too soon to try something like that.'

'You think?' Tania spat out the words. She wanted to go home and curl under her duvet and pretend none of this had happened. More than anything, she was so angry with herself for reacting in this way. *Can't you get a grip? It's just a fall! You didn't break anything! Why are you being such a coward?*

Zac didn't say anything else. Tania knew he was hurt by what she had said, but she couldn't seem to take it back. She started to shiver.

Brock came back with the ice pack and a blanket. 'Here you go. Keep this on your leg in the worst place. Put the blanket round yourself too. You're just a bit shocked, that's all.' He frowned, and Tania knew he was puzzled by her over-reaction. 'It was an accident,' he added gently.

'I *know*, Brock, I'm not stupid!' Tania could hear her own voice straining higher than usual but it was almost as though she were outside herself – there was nothing she could do to change the way she was behaving.

'You should rest,' said Brock.

'What I *should* be doing is practising my singles skating,' snapped Tania. She threw Zac a glance and all the anger, frustration and fear boiled over. 'What is all this for anyway, Brock? It's not helping, can't you see? He's not getting any better and I'm just getting injured. I can't afford to get injured. This is my *career* we're talking about.'

Zac bit his lip. 'Maybe she's right . . .'

'No, she isn't,' said Brock firmly. 'This is just a *bruise*, Tania – you said so yourself. I can't understand why you're so upset about it. You've had injuries before.'

'Yes, but no one *else* has injured me before,' said Tania. 'Any injuries in the past have been my own fault.'

'You have to learn to trust Zac,' said Brock, but Tania interrupted him with a scornful laugh.

'Trust him! He can't even do a simple three turn when he's lifting me! How can I trust him?' She stood up stiffly, clutching the pack to her leg. 'I have to get changed, I'm freezing.'

Brock and Zac watched her limp towards the lockers. She was so upset, she hadn't even put on her skate guards.

Zac looked at Brock. 'I'm not good enough to partner her.'

'You are good enough,' said Brock fiercely.

'But I don't want to be the one who ruins her career,' said Zac. His voice shook slightly. 'She's too good for that. Her skating is way out of my league. And me . . .' He shrugged. 'I never wanted to do this professionally. Maybe it was a bad idea.'

'No.' Brock shook his head. 'This is the right thing for her – for both of you. She'll get over it. She's had worse.' He turned to Zac and smiled, though his eyes were troubled. 'Don't blame yourself. It could happen to anyone.' He paused. 'Though she's right about your basic skills. If you improved those then you'd be far more solid in the complex moves.'

'I'd have to work night and day to get good enough,' muttered Zac, glancing towards the lockers.

Brock looked hard at him. 'You want to be good enough, don't you?'

'Hell, yeah. I'd love to skate as well as her.'

'Then that's what you do. Work day and night. Be here when the rink opens. Be here when it closes. I'll have a word with the staff. It won't cost you any extra.'

Zac looked at him curiously. 'Really? You'd let me come in any time to practise?'

'Any time the ice is available.'

Zac shook his head, puzzled. 'I don't get it. You really think this is going to work?'

Brock took a deep breath. His brow cleared. He glanced towards the locker room and nodded slowly. 'I really do. Don't ask me how or why. I just know it, in my gut.' He turned to Zac. 'Now you go home and get some rest too. You look pretty shaken up.'

'It was scary,' admitted Zac.

Brock patted him on the shoulder. 'Then you've

learned something. A little fear is important. It gives you focus. Tania has too much fear; it's holding her back. But *you'd* try that lift again?'

'Of course.'

Brock nodded again. 'Then Tania can definitely learn from you.'

Chapter 7

I don't want to mess things up for you

Tania sat on the sofa with her leg up on a cushion. It still ached, and a large red patch was developing. Tania knew it would turn black, purple and yellow before it healed fully. The initial shock of the fall had worn off but Tania still felt utterly miserable. She knew she had behaved very badly to Brock and Zac, but she couldn't help feeling angry that Brock had insisted on doing lifts on the ice so soon. Surely he knew it wouldn't help her overcome her fear of falling? At that moment Tania felt as if the whole world were against her.

Caroline brought in a bowl of soup on a tray. 'Chicken,' she said. 'Always good for shock. You still look awfully white, Tania.'

Tania picked up the spoon. 'I'll be all right. I should have known it would happen. It's far too early to be doing lifts on ice.'

'I suppose Brock's trying to fit in as much as he can,' said Caroline. 'Since there isn't much time before the show.'

'It's dangerous,' went on Tania, 'rushing the early stages. We should be working on basic stuff for months before we try anything like that.'

Alistair, Tania's father, came down the stairs. 'Internet's gone off,' he said, annoyed. 'I'm going to have to ring up again.' He looked sympathetically at Tania. 'Feeling better?'

'She thinks Brock's rushing her and Zac into dangerous lifts,' Caroline said.

Alistair raised his eyebrows. 'Really? Doesn't sound like Brock; he's usually very careful.'

'Not this time,' said Tania grumpily. 'It's too soon.'

'But you're good,' said Caroline. 'You should be able to adapt to anything by now.'

'Yes, but *he's* not.' Tania took a mouthful of soup and made a face. 'This is too hot.'

'It's just come out of the saucepan,' said Caroline reasonably. 'It's bound to be hot.'

'It's not going to work out,' said Tania. 'Skating with Zac, I mean. He's good, all right, but he's not up to my standard. Look what happened today! It could have been so much worse.'

'But it wasn't,' said Alistair. 'So let's look on the bright side, OK?'

Tania scowled. But inside she felt like crying. Why couldn't anyone see how scared she was?

Caroline changed the subject. 'Have you finished that geography project yet? I know your teacher was anxious about it.'

Tania put down her spoon in irritation. 'What for? It's only stupid geography.'

'Don't talk like that,' said Caroline. 'School is important. Alistair, tell her.'

'Your mother's right. A good education gets you a step up the career ladder.' He glanced around. 'Where's the phone? Did someone leave it in the kitchen again?'

'I'm not on the career ladder.' Tania sipped her soup again as her father disappeared into the kitchen. 'I'm going to be a competitive skater. I'm not going to get an ordinary job. School is pointless for me.'

'You have a good brain, Tania. Don't waste it.' Caroline frowned. 'You don't get a second chance at school. The rink will always be there.'

'Oh, Mum, we've been through this.' Tania shifted her leg and winced. 'I can't put off skating till I'm older, that's just impossible. It's a young person's sport. I have to do it now, while I still have the chance. And if

I need qualifications later in life, I can get them then.'

'It's not so easy later.'

'Why is everyone interfering!' Tania burst out. 'I just want to skate! Is that too much to ask?' She felt her eyes fill with tears. 'I just want to skate,' she whispered. *I want things to go back to the way they were. Before . . . before . . . that accident.*

Caroline looked at her daughter and felt a pang of sympathy. 'I know, love. I know.' She hesitated for a moment and then took the plunge. 'Have you ever thought what might happen if it isn't possible though? If you just miss out – if you're not quite good enough? What then?'

'What do you mean, not good enough?'

'What if . . .' Caroline swallowed. She knew this was a dangerous question to ask. 'What if *your best* isn't good enough?'

Tania stared at the carpet. She didn't know what to say. The thought had never entered her head that she might not be good enough to compete professionally. What on earth would she do then?

Her mother looked helplessly up at Alistair, standing in the doorway, phone in hand. He shrugged, equally helpless. Sometimes, communicating with Tania was like talking to a brick wall. And yet Caroline was sure there was something else going on. Something that Tania wasn't talking about. But what? And when would she start to open up?

♥

There was no practice the next day for Tania because her leg was so sore. The bruise had indeed come up in a dinner-plate-sized black blob, and Libby was very impressed. 'That's one heck of a bruise, Tan! It must hurt like hell.'

'It does,' said Tania.

'I can't believe he fell on you,' said Libby. 'What an idiot.'

'He didn't mean to,' said Tania.

'Yeah, but still. He should have been more careful.'

'Skating's not a careful sport,' said Tania, trying to navigate the stairs on the way to their next class. 'And Zac's not a careful skater. But it was an accident; it wasn't his fault.'

Libby stopped. 'Hang on a minute. Aren't you mad at him about this? I thought you'd been worrying something like this would happen? You said he was dangerous, after all.'

Tania glanced at the students pouring past. 'Don't stop there, Lib, you're holding everyone up.' She hopped down the last few steps. 'I don't really know *how* I feel, to be honest. I was so angry with him yesterday. I had a real go at Brock about it too. I don't know what's wrong with me – I've had falls before. I completely over-reacted though. I just . . .' She paused. 'I think I'm scared, Libby.'

Libby swung her bag back onto her shoulder. 'Scared of what?'

Tania bit her lip. 'Falling, mostly. Getting hurt. Badly hurt, I mean.'

Libby looked bewildered. 'But why? You're really good. And it's not like it's bothered you before.'

Tania gazed at her best friend. *Tell her. Tell her about Kerri's accident and how badly it shook you up. Tell her about the nightmares you keep having and how it's made you scared of taking risks. Tell her how it's even made you afraid of stepping onto the ice, when it used to be the only thing you wanted to do.*

She opened her mouth. 'I think . . .' she began.

And then the bell rang and Libby's expression changed. 'Argh! We're going to be late for English! Come on! You'll have to tell me later.'

But Tania wasn't sure she'd have the courage later.

♥

To her utter surprise, Tania saw Zac at the school gates. He looked awkward, standing stiffly and running a hand through his spiky blond hair. Tania glanced around. Her mother's car was parked a hundred metres up the road. She could sneak past Zac – he'd never see her in this crowd. But she knew that would be wrong. He must have come to see her, why else would he be here? He didn't attend Parchester County School.

'What are you looking at?' asked Libby, trying to peer past her. 'Your mum's here, isn't she?'

'Yeah, it's just . . .'

'Oh my God,' said Libby suddenly. 'That's *him*, isn't it? That's Zac, right?'

Tania nodded.

Libby's face broke into the most enormous grin Tania had ever seen. 'He's come to see you, to make up.'

'Libby, we haven't broken up, it's not like a date.' Tania tried to say it in a light-hearted way, but the word tasted funny in her mouth. A *date*? What made her say that?

'You know what I mean.' Libby nudged her. 'Go on, go and say hi. He's probably brought flowers or something.'

'Of course he hasn't, you can see from here.'

Libby wasn't put off. 'All right, chocolates then. In his pocket.'

Tania rolled her eyes.

Libby nudged her again. 'Go on, go over, for goodness' sake. He is so *cute*, Tania. Why didn't you tell me he was cute?'

'Libby . . .'

'I'll tell your mum you'll just be a minute, OK?' Libby skipped off, turning to mouth 'Good luck!' as she reached the gates.

Tania took a deep breath. Automatically she smoothed down her hair. Did she look OK? It had been a long day at school . . . 'Oh, for goodness' sake!' she said out loud. 'He's not my *boyfriend*!'

A couple of people turned to look at her curiously but Tania had set off towards Zac.

He grinned at her when she came into view, but it was a half-grin, an uncertain grin. 'Hi,' he said. 'How are you?'

'What are you doing here?' asked Tania abruptly, and then bit her tongue. 'Sorry. I didn't mean to sound rude.'

'That's OK,' said Zac. He looked around. 'Busy, isn't it? Can we go somewhere to talk? Just for a minute?'

Tania glanced over to her mum's car. Libby was leaning in the passenger window and having an animated conversation with Caroline. Something inside her tingled. It was the first time she'd seen Zac outside the rink. It was like two worlds colliding and it felt strange. 'All right,' she said. 'I haven't got long though.'

They walked round the corner towards the little green with its park benches. Schoolkids were already occupying most of them, flicking bits of paper at each other, but Zac sat down on one of the benches, and after a moment, the kids moved off, casting annoyed glances back at him. Tania sat down next to him.

'I came to say sorry,' said Zac. 'For dropping you yesterday. I really am sorry – I was so mad at myself.'

'It was an accident,' said Tania.

'Yeah, but it shouldn't have happened,' said Zac. 'I was sloppy on my outside edge. You were right about my basic skills not being up to scratch.' He took a breath. 'I wanted to say I understand if you don't want to do this any more. I know you've had a bit of a hard time recently. I guess yesterday didn't help much.'

Tania twisted her fingers together. 'Not really.'

'Brock seemed to think you needed to let go a bit on the ice,' said Zac. 'He said you were getting too tight, needed to take a few risks. But if the first time you take a risk, someone else drops you, then you're not going to feel any happier about it.'

He understands! Tania felt warmth sweep through her. 'No, not really.'

Zac turned to face her. 'If you feel you don't want to skate with me any more, then it's OK. I understand. I'll tell Brock. You don't have to feel bad about it.'

Tania frowned. 'Well . . .' He was offering her a way out. She should take it. Shouldn't she?

'Hang on a sec,' said Zac. 'Before you make up your mind, I just wanted to say something.' He chewed his lip for a moment. 'I'd really like to carry on skating with you,' he said in a rush. 'I know I'm not up to your standard, but I'm really enjoying it, and I am improving. Just keeping up with you in practice sessions is making me work harder than ever before!'

Tania felt her mouth twitch.

Zac went on. 'If you give me a week – just a week – I'll prove I can do better. You'll need to rest for a few days anyway, because of what I did to you.' He pulled a face. 'So give me that time to work on my basic skills. Brock says I can go to the rink whenever I like.'

'What about school?' said Tania, before realizing she didn't even know if he *was* still at school.

'College,' said Zac. 'I'm at Bartholomew's. It's OK, I can miss a few lessons. I can catch up at home. Skating is more important.'

Tania gave a small smile. 'I thought skating was just fun for you.'

Zac looked at her. 'It is. But I don't want to mess things up for *you*. I want to do it right. It's important to me.'

Tania caught his gaze, and something inside her felt reassured. He looked sincere. 'I do believe you . . .' she said slowly. 'It's just . . .'

'You're scared I'll drop you again,' said Zac. He nodded. 'It's OK, I know. I would be too.' He rubbed his nose. 'Listen, Tania. I can't promise I'll never drop you again. That would be stupid. But I can promise I will work harder than I have been. I want to be a good partner.'

Tania felt embarrassed. Why was the warmth creeping up her cheeks?

Zac was still staring earnestly at her. 'I think you're an amazing skater, Tania. I haven't said it before. Just watching what you can do – wow. I feel privileged to be skating with you. Give me another chance. Please.'

Tania's cheeks were red-hot. She attempted a laugh. 'What can I say?' she said, trying to hide her embarrassment. 'I guess so.'

Zac sat back. 'Thank you. Just give me a week, that's all. If after that you still think it's not going to work, we'll both go and tell Brock. OK?'

'OK.'

He grinned at her, a full-hearted grin this time, and Tania felt her stomach flip. *What on earth is going on?* she wondered. *Why is talking to him suddenly making you blush like some besotted girl – like Libby, for example?*

'See you in a few days,' he said and got up. 'Not too soon – rest the leg.'

'All right.' Tania watched him until he was out of sight. Then she picked up her bag and got painfully to her feet. Her legs felt a bit weak, but she told herself that was because of the bruising.

A little girl blew a gum bubble at her as she passed. 'You fancy him,' she said to Tania.

'Do not,' Tania threw over her shoulder as she limped on.

'I would,' said the girl. 'He's gorgeous!'

Chapter 8

butterflies

Tania was off the ice for four days in the end, and she had no idea what to do with herself. Her mother was in despair. 'Haven't you got homework or something?' she asked. 'That geography project you were supposed to hand in ages ago, what about that?'

Tania shrugged. 'Done it.' She flicked channels on the TV. 'It's rubbish but at least it's done. And Mr Craven knows I hate his subject.'

Caroline sighed. 'I wish you would make a bit more effort sometimes. If you tried a bit harder you might even find you enjoy it.'

'Not geography. It's boring.'

Her mother's lips pressed together. Having Tania at home was making it even harder to get on with her than usual. 'Are you going to ballet tomorrow?'

'Miss Stewart told me not to come because of my leg,' said Tania. 'I rang her earlier and she said best to rest it for as long as I can.' She got up off the sofa. 'It's much better now though. But Brock told me not to go in till the day after tomorrow.' She cast a look at the window, where the darkening skies predicted rain. 'Can't even go out.'

'What about Libby?' asked Caroline. 'Could you go round and see her? Or have her come here?'

'She's out with her parents,' said Tania. 'Her mum's birthday.'

'Oh,' said Caroline, falling silent. It was always like this when Tania couldn't go skating. She moped around the house like a gloomy thundercloud, snapping at everyone. It was almost as though, without skating, Tania wasn't a whole person. She needed it to keep going and, without it, she didn't know what to do with herself. But instead of being able to amuse herself quietly with a book or the TV, she was constantly bothering her mother, asking her what she was doing, whether she could have new tights, what she thought of taking the next NISA test in the spring. Caroline found herself trying to amuse her daughter in the same way she had when Tania was a small child: 'Why don't you draw a picture? Write a story? Help me make these new curtains?' And, just as it had been when Tania was little, none of these suggestions went down well and there were half-finished projects all over the house.

In the end, Caroline gave up trying to achieve anything herself and when Tania's father came back from work, they all played Cluedo and had a Chinese takeaway.

Tania cheered up a bit during the game, but her parents noticed how quiet she became towards the end, as though her mind were somewhere else entirely. Her father even waved a hand in front of her face at one point. 'Earth to Tania? It's your turn.'

'What? Oh, sorry.'

'Penny for your thoughts?' asked Caroline.

Tania shook her head. 'Nothing. Just – you know.'

'Skating?' suggested Alistair.

'Sort of.'

Her parents exchanged glances. 'It must be difficult for you, being away from the rink like this,' commented Alistair.

Tania wriggled. 'It's sort of like an itch. I want to get back but I don't, if you see what I mean.'

Alistair raised his eyebrows. 'That's the first time I've heard you say you're not keen to get back to it.'

'But I am. I really want to get on with my training. Oh, I don't know. Can we talk about something else?'

Her mother paused for a moment. 'Of course. How about Mrs Peacock in the Library with the lead piping?'

Later, Tania lay in bed and thought about the rink. She did want to get back to it – so much. It was as though every day she spent away from it was somehow painful. And of course there was Zac too. Despite her scornful opinion of his technical skills, Tania kind of missed seeing him. He was so open, so totally honest with her. It surprised her because she knew she had put up so many emotional barriers herself. Being with Zac was refreshing and she knew she would be pleased to see him again.

But she also knew that when she returned to the ice, so would the fear. The fear of falling.

A crack of bone, a high scream . . .

Tania turned over in bed and wondered if she would ever feel completely happy about skating again.

♥

As she laced up her boots, Tania had butterflies in her stomach. The bruise on her thigh was gradually healing, but it was still painful to the touch. At least the leg felt stronger.

Tania couldn't help wondering whether Zac had

been as good as his word. He'd said he wanted to improve enough to skate with her – but did he really mean it or was he just saying it to persuade her not to give up skating with him? She told herself the butterflies in her stomach were entirely to do with her own skating and nothing to do with Zac, but when she saw him walking towards her, several of the butterflies seemed to fly straight up into her throat. Libby was right; he *was* cute.

'Hi,' said Zac, smiling at her. 'You look a lot better. How's the leg?'

'Getting there.'

He held out his hand. 'You ready?'

Tania noticed he still had on his broken-down boots, but she didn't say anything. Instead, she took his hand with a nod.

'No gloves?' Zac said in surprise.

Tania shook her head. 'Think they were getting in the way.' His hand felt strong and warm, and another butterfly did a triple loop. *What on earth is happening to me?* she wondered. *I've never had this kind of reaction to a boy before!*

As soon as they stepped onto the ice, Tania could feel a difference in Zac. His skating was stronger; more confident. As they worked their way around the rink in back crossovers, her surprise grew. His edges were much cleaner, and although the old blades still scraped on the ice, his posture was a lot more solid.

When they stopped for a moment, Tania turned to Zac. 'You *have* been practising!'

He grinned. 'Told you.'

She shook her head. 'I can't believe there's such a difference in four days. What have you been doing?'

'Basic skills. All day, every day.'

'*All day?*'

'Well, whenever I could get onto the ice. Brock's been helping me out.' Zac nodded towards the end of the rink, and Tania saw Brock leaning over the side and smiling at them.

'Quite a difference, isn't there?' he called.

Tania skated over. 'Has he *really* been here all day every day?' she asked in a low voice.

Brock nodded. 'Yup. And he's finally started listening to what I've been telling him for the last two years.'

Zac, joining them, heard this and grinned. 'It's the first time I've had a reason to,' he said cheekily.

'Right,' said Brock. 'So then. Lifts.'

Tania felt something in her tense up, but she was determined that Zac and Brock shouldn't see her nerves. 'Let's do it.'

They practised for over an hour, doing the basic lifts again and again. Brock seemed pleased, but Tania knew she wasn't doing as well as she should. Zac was a lot steadier under her, but Tania had skated alone for years. It just wasn't that easy to trust someone else to carry her across the ice. Especially with that nagging panic of falling. 'Again,' Brock kept saying, and Tania knew it was because of her.

Zac was patient, but she could tell he was puzzled. She felt angry with herself. Why couldn't she just relax and trust him? She knew he would never drop her on purpose. The last time had been a complete accident; it could have happened to anyone. She had been telling herself that this time would be different, now that Zac had proved how keen he was to work hard. Surely she could overcome this one little problem? But every time they were speeding across the ice and Brock said, 'Prepare . . .' Tania knew every muscle in her body was tightening, and not in a good way. Her heart sank as the hour wore on.

'Now.' Brock looked from one to the other. 'The death spiral.' The death spiral was a required element in pairs skating, and it always drew applause from the crowd. Done properly, it was a masterpiece of aesthetics, the female skater bent backwards over the ice, one blade only skimming the surface, whilst her partner held her by the hand and twirled her around him in a huge circle.

Brock explained the preparation for the spiral, and how Tania needed to get herself into the correct position. He even made her lie down on the ice to start with, so that Zac could try spinning her around him. But as soon as they began practising, Tania tensed up.

'Loosen your back,' called Brock. 'You're not leaning back far enough.'

'I'll fall.'

'No you won't,' said Brock. 'Zac's holding you.'

'I won't drop you,' Zac told her. Tania looked at him. She believed him – at least, she believed that he believed it – but she just couldn't do it. The position meant her head was only inches from the ice as it whistled past underneath her. They tried again, and again Tania chickened out.

'I'm sorry. I just can't.'

Zac looked at Brock, and Brock looked at Tania. 'Look,' said Brock. 'I understand you're nervous. But this isn't about Zac. This is about *you*. It's the same problem that you're having with the jumps. You're too tight. You've *got* to loosen up.'

'Yes, I know, I know!' said Tania, annoyed with herself. 'It's not as if you haven't said it enough.'

'It's no good snapping at me,' said Brock, starting to get annoyed too. 'You've been tensing up all session. Every time you have to take a risk. What exactly is the problem?'

Tania shook her head miserably. She couldn't tell them. What would they think if she admitted that an accident that happened to someone else six months ago was making her terrified to skate? It would be so humiliating. She could just imagine the pity on Zac's face. She didn't want pity. She was strong; had always been strong. No, she would struggle on by herself. 'Nothing. I don't know.'

'It won't do, Tania.'

'I *am* trying.'

'Well, trying's not good enough,' said Brock bluntly. 'It's time to get over it. Zac's been working hard to come up to your standard. He's made incredible progress in such a short space of time. He deserves better from you.'

'Oh, well . . .' said Zac, looking uncomfortable. 'That's not exactly . . .'

'If this pairs programme doesn't work,' said Brock, 'it'll be because of you, Tania – not Zac. You've got to learn to let go.'

'Maybe you're thinking too much,' suggested Zac. She could tell he was trying to be kind. 'You think you're going to fall, so you're more likely to. If you see what I mean. Maybe you should think about something else as we go into the lift.'

Tania looked at him in despair. 'Think about something *else*? Are you kidding?'

'Time's up,' said Brock. He looked hard at Tania. 'This is a real mental block for you. It's time we tried something different.'

Tania's heart thumped. 'Like what?'

'I don't know,' Brock said, frowning. 'But I'll give it some thought. I'm not here tomorrow, so you two practise without me. I'll leave you instructions.'

'All right.'

'Hey,' Zac touched Tania's arm as they set off to the lockers. 'I'm sorry. I guess I'm not helping as much as Brock hoped I would.'

'I just don't know what else to do,' Tania said miserably. 'I am trying to let go, I really am.' *But I can't. For once in my life, my body won't do what my head is telling it*.

'I know. You're used to being in control.'

Tania thought for a moment. 'On the ice, I am. It's the only place where it's just me, you know? Everything I do on the ice – I do it all by myself. I control it. Outside the rink – school, my family, where I go, what I eat – everything is planned for me.'

Zac raised his eyebrows. 'Sounds like skating is supposed to be an escape for you.'

'It's not quite like that.' She looked at him suddenly. 'Meet me upstairs, by the front entrance, after you've got changed. There's something I want to show you.'

Zac was waiting, his skate bag slung over his shoulder. Tania nodded to his left. 'You see that?' It was a big glass case full of trophies, cups and shields.

Zac turned. 'Seen it every day. What about it?'

'Look at the names on the cups.'

Zac put his bag on the floor and bent to the cabinet to look more closely. *Junior Freestyle: Tania Dunn. Highest Achievement in Short Programme: Tania Dunn. Junior Skater of the Year: Tania Dunn. Silver Medal, Annual Competition: Tania Dunn. Gold Medal, Winter Ice Competition: Tania Dunn.* There were other names too, but Tania's occurred more often than any other.

Zac whistled. 'That's a lot of trophies.'

'I know. And it's sort of what I was saying downstairs. They're mine – I won them all by myself. I didn't have to depend on anyone else, it was all me. I have a real track record. I *like* winning. But these are mostly in the Junior sections. I need to break into the Seniors. I have to if I want a serious career. I want to compete at the World Championships. I want to compete at the Olympics. I want to win them all. And it's easier to do it on my own. That way I don't have to rely on anyone else.'

Zac gave her a long look. Then he took a breath and said, 'Is that what it's all about, though? Winning trophies?'

'What do you mean?'

'I mean this' – Zac waved his hand – 'it's all very impressive, but all it means is that you're good at winning trophies.'

'I don't understand what you're talking about. If I'm winning trophies, then I'm the best. I *have* to be the best.'

'Why?'

Tania was stumped. 'What do you mean, why?'

'What's it for?'

'To prove I'm good. To prove I'm not just a child skater.'

'Prove to who?'

Tania gave a laugh. 'Everyone, of course!'

Zac nodded slowly. 'But don't you do it because you love it? I mean, what's the point in winning if you're not happy?'

Tania bit her lip. 'Winning *makes* me happy. And I know I'm not good enough to win at the moment. That's why I have to train so hard – to get better, so I can win.'

'But what if you couldn't win? Would you still do it?' persisted Zac. 'I mean, do you love it just for what it is, or only because you can collect trophies?'

'I love it, of course . . .' Tania started to say, but her voice trailed off. Was that really true? If she didn't beat this fear, if she couldn't compete any more, would she want to carry on skating?

Zac was watching her closely. 'You used to love it, didn't you?' he said in a soft voice. Tania swallowed and nodded. 'So what happened? Why has it changed?'

Tania felt tears prick her eyes at his gentle tone. 'Something happened a while back . . .' she replied, but her voice wobbled and she clamped her lips shut.

Zac waited, but she didn't say any more. 'It must have been bad,' he said gently. 'To change the way you feel so much. It's OK, you don't have to tell me.'

But I want to, Tania thought. *I want to so much. But I'm even more afraid of what you'll say if I do.*

For a brief moment, Zac's eyes met hers in the reflective glass of the cabinet. 'You know I'll help if I can,' he said. 'If you ever want to talk.'

A tear slid from Tania's eye. She brushed it away, clearing her throat. 'I'll be fine. Thanks, but I can sort it out myself.'

He paused for a moment. *Please go away*, Tania

thought silently. *You're just making things worse by being so kind.*

Zac sighed. 'OK. See you tomorrow.'

'Yeah.'

She didn't dare turn until she heard the front doors bang shut, in case he saw her crying.

Chapter 9

you *are* falling for him!

Brock was as good as his word, and when Tania arrived at the rink the next morning for their six a.m. practice, there was an envelope addressed to her and Zac waiting at the front desk. Tania had had a stern talk to herself the night before. *Stop falling apart*, she'd told herself. *Things will be fine. You just have to keep working through it. And stop thinking about what Zac said and wishing you'd told him everything. He doesn't want to skate with a wet blanket. Put your head up and smile cheerfully*. So that's what she'd done. And she was relieved he hadn't mentioned the day before or asked her how she was feeling.

'Wonder what fiendish idea he's had?' said Zac as Tania picked up the envelope.

She tore it open. 'Only one way to find out.' Heads bent over the letter, they read:

Dear Tania and Zac

I have been thinking a lot about our particular problems. Tania, you know you tense up whenever you do something remotely dangerous. Zac, you know your skating lacks finesse and elegance. So I have devised two activities for you both to undertake this weekend.

On Saturday you will both attend a two-hour ballet workshop at the Parchester Apollo with a visiting company. Meet at the stage Door on Broughton Street at 9.30 a.m. After the class I have arranged for you to watch the ballet rehearsal in the afternoon and I hope you will take advantage of this opportunity.

On Sunday come to the rink at 10 a.m. and you will both be taken by minibus to SkyJumpers, an outdoor pursuits place in Whitstable Wood. SkyJumpers specializes in high-wire activities such as abseiling, climbing and zip-wires. You will be back by 5 p.m.

These two activity days should give you both a fresh outlook on your skating, and I expect to see you as usual on Monday with new attitudes and new skills to put into practice.

I have cleared all of this with your parents.
Best wishes
Brock
PS Don't even think about backing out.

Zac's eyes were shining. 'SkyJumpers, fantastic!'

Tania felt sick. High-wire activities! Abseiling! The chance to fall and break her neck from a great height, even more dangerous than skating! 'I can't,' she muttered.

Zac thumped her on the back. 'Course you can. You'll be harnessed up and everything, it isn't like you have to jump without a safety net. I can't wait! It's going to be so cool!'

Tania's panic made her retort, 'You've got to get through the *ballet* class first.'

Zac's face fell. 'All that girly stuff,' he said. 'Pointing your toes and that.'

'And tights,' added Tania, secretly pleased to see his discomfort.

He looked horrified. 'They won't!'

'They will,' said Tania, starting to feel a little better. At least ballet was something she knew well. 'Tights and leotard.'

Zac glanced down at himself. 'I don't have the body for that kind of gear.'

Tania bit back a reply, flushed, and turned away to avoid any kind of embarrassment. It had just occurred to her that she wouldn't mind seeing Zac in leotard and tights at all!

♥

Libby was depressed. 'Connor Murphy is going out with Alice Fisher.'

'Oh, Lib.' Tania put an arm around her friend. 'Sorry. I know you liked him.'

'Yeah, well,' said Libby. 'If he's too stupid to see what's right under his nose . . . and Alice Fisher! She's just so – *obvious*.'

'You want to hear something crazy?' asked Tania.

'What sort of crazy?'

'Zac and I are going to a ballet workshop tomorrow.'

Libby's jaw dropped. 'He's going to *ballet*? How did you manage that?'

'I didn't.' Tania grinned. 'Brock did. He says Zac's skating needs more elegance, so he's sending him to ballet and I'm going too.'

'Has he ever been to ballet before?'

'Nope.'

Libby laughed. 'Sounds like it could be a disaster.'

'I don't know.' Tania looked thoughtful. 'He's very strong, Lib. Toned, I mean.'

'Toned? As in *muscles*?' Libby's eyes lit up. 'And how would you know *that*, Tania Dunn?'

Tania ignored the flush creeping up her face. 'Because, you idiot, every time he lifts me, I can feel the muscles.'

'Mmm, muscles . . .' Libby wiped imaginary drool from the corner of her mouth. 'Yummy. Oh my God!' She grabbed Tania's arm. 'Is he going to be in – you know – ballet clothes too? Tights and stuff? Pink shoes?'

'Men wear black shoes, Lib,' said Tania, amused. 'But yes, I expect he'll be in tights and leotard. They're a professional company; they wouldn't let him do the class in trackie bottoms.'

Libby stared at her. 'And how do you feel about that? Seeing Zac in skimpy clothing?'

Tania shrugged, trying to pretend the image hadn't played in her mind all night. 'Fine. Nothing weird about it.'

'Yeah, *right*.' Libby brought her face up to Tania's. 'You haven't stopped thinking about it since you heard, have you?'

Tania squirmed. 'All right. I have thought about it a bit.'

'I *knew* it!' Libby yelped. 'You *are* falling for him! You can't fool me! Go on, Tan, you can tell me. I'm your best friend. Do you fancy him? Do you? Do you?'

Tania laughed and fought her off. 'Leave me alone! You are obsessed!'

Libby sat back down. 'Seriously, though, Tania. Are you – you know . . . ?'

Tania chewed her thumbnail. 'I don't know. A bit, I suppose. He is nice. Nicer than I thought. But I don't know anything about him.'

'You're spending hours with him!'

'But we don't talk about ourselves. We're skating. We talk about edges and sequences and things like that.'

Libby looked thoughtful. 'Well, maybe tomorrow you'll have a bit more time. What about Sunday, are you meeting to practise then?'

'No.' Tania suddenly shivered. 'We're going to SkyJumpers.'

'Sky whattie?'

'SkyJumpers. It's that place out in Whitstable Wood, you know, with the high wires and rope bridges.'

Libby stared at her. 'Why are you going there?'

'It's this other thing Brock's organized,' said Tania. 'Ballet on Saturday, to improve Zac's posture. SkyJumpers on Sunday to give me more confidence to do dangerous things.'

'Wow.'

'Yeah.'

'You don't look too thrilled.'

'I'm not.' Tania burst out, 'Oh, Libby, it's going to be horrendous! I hate all that extreme sports stuff!'

Libby laughed. 'You're a championship *skater*, Tan. It's not exactly the tamest thing to do! Why on earth would you be scared of rope bridges and things like that?'

'What if I fall? What if I injure myself and I can't skate any more?'

'Don't be daft, there'll be loads of health-and-safety things like helmets and harnesses. They won't let you fall.'

'How am I going to be able to face it though?' Tania looked agonized. 'How am I even going to be able to walk into the place?'

Libby patted her on the shoulder. 'Hold Zac's hand, of course. And think about his muscles instead.'

Tania's expression relaxed under Libby's eager gaze. Amused, she said, 'I don't think that will help.'

Libby nodded. 'Oh it will. Trust me.'

♥

At 9.25 a.m. on Saturday, Tania was standing nervously outside the Apollo stage door. She had brought everything she could possibly need for the day –

dancewear, ballet shoes, packed lunch, water bottle, hairbrush . . .

'Could you not find a bigger bag?' said Zac, eyeing her enormous shoulder bag when he arrived.

'How did you manage to fit everything into *that*?' asked Tania, prodding Zac's empty-looking rucksack.

He shrugged. 'Leotard, tights, shoes. What else would I need?'

Tania smirked. 'Where did you get them?'

'Borrowed them,' said Zac shortly, and Tania was delighted to see a slight flush to his cheeks. 'My mum rang this ballet teacher friend of hers – Corinne. She lent them to me. Didn't think I'd be allowed in otherwise.'

'Speaking of which,' said Tania, 'we'd better go in.'

The stage door manager directed them to a rehearsal room on the first floor, and Tania and Zac were surprised to see several other young people limbering up outside. 'I thought this was just for us,' whispered Zac.

One of the girls, clad in a peacock-coloured leotard, looked up. 'It's a general workshop,' she said. 'Didn't you read the info?'

'We didn't arrange it,' said Tania hastily. 'Someone else did.'

'You were lucky,' said the peacock girl. 'Places

got snapped up really quickly. They are the Ballet *Formidable*, after all.' She said this in such an impressed tone of voice that Zac and Tania exchanged glances.

'Wonder how Brock managed to wangle this one?' murmured Zac.

'We'd better get changed.'

'Girls' changing is down there.' The peacock girl pointed. 'Boys' is on the next floor up.'

'See you in a minute,' said Zac, and ran lightly up the stairs.

The peacock girl followed Tania into the changing rooms and went straight to a bag hanging on a peg. 'He's cute,' she said casually, fishing out a hairbrush, even though her hair was already scraped back into an immaculate bun. 'He your boyfriend?'

'No,' said Tania shortly. 'He – um – we skate together.'

'What, like inlining?'

'No, ice skating.'

The peacock girl sat down on the bench. 'I'm Suki,' she said, 'by the way.'

'Tania.'

'Ice skating, wow,' said Suki. 'I always wanted to do ice skating but my ballet teacher said it would be bad for my knees.' She picked hairs out of the brush.

Tania swiftly got out of her outdoor clothes and wriggled into her tights. 'Bad for your knees? I never heard that before.'

Suki shrugged. 'My teacher used to be professional. With the Birmingham Royal Ballet. She would know.'

Tania kept quiet. She was sure Suki would be quite happy to provide most of the conversation.

Suki put the unused hairbrush back in her bag and reached for a pot of lip gloss. 'So if you're an ice skater, what are you doing here?'

'My coach booked the workshop,' said Tania.

'Oh, right. Because my friend wanted to come but she was told there weren't any more places. And this was weeks ago.'

'Oh dear.' Tania didn't dare mention that Brock had only booked the class a couple of days previously.

'We're both going to the Rambert open workshop next week,' Suki went on. 'My friend and me. My teacher says they look out for potential new members there.'

'Oh, do they?' Tania flicked her leotard straps over her shoulders, wishing Suki would go away.

'But of course I'd rather join the English National,' said Suki. 'Or the Royal.'

'Don't you have to train at the Royal Ballet School for that?'

Suki shot her a look of pure venom. 'Some people don't mature until later,' she said coldly.

'Pardon?' Tania was baffled.

'I'm going to audition again next year,' Suki told her.

'Again?'

'I didn't get a place at eleven,' said Suki, as if the words tasted nasty in her mouth. 'But I only just missed out, they told me. My feet have developed since then.'

'Oh.'

Suki looked Tania up and down. 'Is that what you're wearing?'

Tania glanced down at her pale pink tights, plum-coloured leotard, warm-up leggings and leather ballet shoes. 'Yes, why?'

'No reason.' Suki got up. 'We'd better go in.'

Tania followed her down the corridor, hoping the class would be so busy she wouldn't have to talk to Suki again. She glanced around but saw no sign of Zac. Hadn't he finished changing yet?

The doors to the rehearsal room opened, and a young woman stuck her head out. 'You all here for the workshop? Do come in and warm up – we'll get going in a minute.'

Tania followed the others in, still wondering where

Zac could have got to. 'Is it always like this?' a voice muttered in her ear, and she turned in surprise. 'Zac! I didn't recognize you!'

Zac grinned sheepishly. 'Yeah, well, I'm not exactly in my usual clothes, am I?'

Tania took in the broad chest, the bare well-defined arms, and swallowed. She didn't dare look down. 'You look fine,' she said.

Zac squirmed. 'These tights go up my . . . I mean, are they *supposed* to do that?'

Tania stifled a laugh.

'Hi there.' Suki suddenly appeared at Tania's side. 'I gather you're Tania's ice-skating partner?'

'Uh – yeah,' said Zac. 'Do you know Tania?'

'Oh, we're old friends,' said Suki, with a giggle. Tania stared at her in disbelief. *How* annoying was this girl? 'I'm Suki.'

'Zac.'

'Zac – what a cool name. Is it short for Isaac?'

'Yeah.'

Tania looked at him in astonishment. She had never even thought about Zac's real name! He caught her eye and looked away in embarrassment. 'Don't tell anyone.'

'Oh, but Isaac is a great name,' said Suki, slipping her arm through Zac's. 'So strong.'

Tania felt annoyed. Who was this girl anyway? And why was she attaching herself to Zac so persuasively? And, more to the point, why wasn't Zac shaking her off?

Thankfully, at that moment, six dancers from the Ballet *Formidable* came in and the workshop began.

Tania enjoyed herself. Basic exercises like *pliés* and *tendus* came easily to her, and she was congratulated by one of the dancers on the control of her *battements*. Suki glowered at her from the other end of the barre.

Every now and then, Tania glanced across at Zac. It was obvious to everyone that he wasn't used to the technique. One of the male dancers was soon permanently at his side, correcting his turnout and reminding him of his posture. But Zac was taking all criticism very cheerfully, and Tania couldn't help but notice the strength and shape of his legs. Dance tights were very revealing!

'Focus, Tania,' said one of the dancers, and Tania blushed, looking away from Zac and concentrating on her *port de bras*.

After the first forty minutes, the dancers called a short break, and Zac headed straight for Tania. 'This is hard work!' he said, wiping his face. 'I didn't realize it would be like going to the gym – I should have brought a towel.'

'I've got one you can borrow,' said Tania. She fetched it from the changing room. When she came back, she was annoyed to see Suki talking to Zac again. 'So you've not been skating that long?' she was saying. 'And can already do all those jumps? You must be really talented!'

Zac looked a little uncomfortable. 'I practise . . .' he mumbled. 'And I'm not nearly as talented as Tania.'

Tania felt a blush creep up her cheeks.

'Oh, really?' asked Suki, though she looked as though she'd just sucked on a lemon.

'She's amazing,' went on Zac. 'But now I've been in a class like this, I can see why. She must have put in so much extra work to get that good.' He caught sight of Tania out of the corner of his eye and grinned.

Tania felt confused. Wasn't he embarrassed? He must know she'd just heard everything he said! 'Uh – here's that towel.'

'Thanks,' said Zac gratefully, wiping his face and arms. 'I was just telling Suki what a great skater you are.'

Tania mumbled something like, 'Yeah, I heard . . .'

'Yes,' said Suki, looking unenthusiastic. 'But go back to what you were saying about the jumps.' She turned pointedly away from Tania. 'What were you telling me about a triple something-or-other? The one that sounds like judo?'

'Salchow.' Zac laughed. 'It does sound like a martial art.'

The dancers called time on the break. Her head buzzing, Tania went to take her place at the barre. Did Zac really think she was that good? Of course, Tania knew she was a good skater, but somehow the thought that Zac admired her made her feel slightly dizzy. She reached out for the barre to steady herself. 'Not this time,' called Pierre, one of the dancers. 'Now we do centre and floor work.'

There was no more opportunity for Tania to muse over the way Zac might or might not feel about her. The rest of the workshop required all her concentration and effort to keep up. Curiously, though, Zac seemed to have hit his stride. At one point, Pierre called the rest of them over to look at Zac's *grand jétés*. 'See what elevation he gets,' said Pierre admiringly. 'In ballet, detail is not enough. You need power too.'

Tania watched Zac leap across the room and felt a strange tingling of pride. Then she glanced sideways and saw Suki watching with such a look of adoration on her face, Tania felt quite sick.

'Of course, you need to match power with beauty,' said Pierre, after congratulating Zac, who looked flushed but pleased. 'And although Zac has the power to leap that high, his turnout and arms could be better. Lines are important. Arabesque in the air is what we're looking for.' He glanced around. 'Can I have someone to demonstrate an arabesque please?'

Suki's hand shot up, but Natasha, one of Pierre's fellow dancers, pointed at Tania. 'She has very nice lines.'

'Out you come,' said Pierre, beckoning.

Tania went pink, but she was determined not to mess up in front of Suki, who looked as angry as a thundercloud. 'Third arabesque,' said Pierre. 'With the feeling of longing.'

'The feeling of . . . ?' said Tania, confused.

Pierre tried to explain. 'Imagine there is something you want – something just out of reach. Keep that in mind as you hold your arabesque.'

Tania took up her position, breathed deeply, lifted her back leg and leaned forward, gazing fixedly at the window and trying desperately to think of something other than Zac. Skating – she wanted to be a singles skater – she loved the ice, didn't she? But between the images of the rink was Zac's face, pushing its way into her consciousness. His eyes, the way the tiny golden flecks in them caught the light; the way they crinkled at the edges when he smiled. Something she wanted . . . ?

A hush fell over the room.

'Beautiful,' murmured Pierre, and there was a whisper of agreement from the other dancers.

Tania felt her whole body tingling. This was what it was like on the ice – or how it used to be. People watching, and all the time her knowing that she was achieving something special. Her fingers seemed to lengthen as she reached out to the thing she wanted; her toes stretched away from her, but her whole body felt weightless. She held the arabesque for a long time, but it was almost as if the moment had frozen.

'Thank you, Tania,' Pierre said finally, and she came out of the position, her body suddenly stiff and achy from having held it for so long.

'So in Zac we have power,' said Pierre, 'and in Tania we have beauty. But in ballet you must have both. And so now we are going to teach you a routine from our production of *Hansel and Gretel* that you will find challenging, both physically and emotionally. For as you saw from Tania's arabesque, the feeling is paramount. Without the thought behind the movement, there is no beauty.'

Pierre organized them into small groups, and Zac

sidled over to Tania. 'That was *awesome*. It was like you existed on another plane or something.'

'I haven't ever done it quite like that before,' Tania whispered back. 'It did feel different.'

'I could see that. What were you thinking about?'

Tania was flummoxed. What could she say? 'Skating,' she stammered.

Zac nodded. 'Then you do love it after all. I could see it in your whole body.'

Tania mumbled something incomprehensible.

Chapter 10

you were really good

'That wasn't so bad after all,' Zac said, as they left the rehearsal room, dripping with sweat. 'I quite enjoyed it.'

'You were really good,' said Tania sincerely. 'I didn't think you'd do so well. You were so controlled.'

'Not how I am on the ice?' grinned Zac. 'You're right. Ballet is a lot more about control and precision. It's a bit alien to me.'

'But you made real progress,' said Tania.

'Zac!' Suki came bursting out of the rehearsal room. 'A few of us are going to grab a bite to eat at the pizza place on the corner. You want to come?'

The invitation very obviously didn't include Tania. Zac glanced at Tania. 'Uh, well . . .' She glared at him. Zac hastily said, 'Sorry, Suki. Me and Tania are staying on for the afternoon rehearsal.' Tania smiled sweetly at Suki, inwardly delighted at the look on her face.

'You're what?' Suki stared. 'What do you mean?'

'Our coach arranged for us to watch the rehearsal this afternoon,' said Tania in an airy tone. Then she pretended to look surprised. 'Oh, didn't it say that in the *info*? Never mind, I'm sure *you'll* be able to see the show one evening or something.'

Zac snorted. Suki gave Tania a glare that clearly said 'I wish you were dead' and stalked off. Tania laughed.

'How long have you known her?' asked Zac.

'I just met her today.'

'No way! She said the two of you were old friends.' Zac raised his eyebrows. 'Why didn't you say something?'

Tania shrugged. 'What for? She wasn't interested in anything *I* said.' She felt unusually bold. 'She only had eyes for *you*.' *How is he going to respond to that?*

Zac looked surprised for a moment, and then he grinned. 'Yeah, she did, didn't she?'

'Don't get all big-headed about it.' Tania tried to sound confident but inside she was anxious. *Does he fancy her?*

'She's quite pretty . . .' mused Zac, as though thinking hard.

'She is not! Her legs are too short and her nose is too big!' spluttered Tania.

Zac roared with laughter. '*Miaow*! Remember how I said you were so easy to wind up?'

'*Oh!*' Tania made a noise of exasperation. Now she felt stupid! 'I'm going for a shower. So I'll have *that* back please.' She snatched the towel from his hands and headed off to the changing rooms, leaving Zac chuckling behind her.

♥

'We need to find somewhere for lunch,' said Zac, when they met again.

'You're still all wet!' said Tania, seeing the rivulets of water drip off his hair and down his neck.

Zac rolled his eyes. 'What do you expect when you don't have a towel?'

'Oh.'

'Now I'm sure you brought your own sandwiches and all that . . .' Zac raised his eyebrows and smirked when Tania looked down, 'but I didn't, so let's go find some food.'

'Not pizza.'

Zac laughed again. 'All right, not pizza.'

They settled on a small café just next to the theatre.

'So why didn't you do ballet instead of skating?' asked Zac as he bit hungrily into a panini. 'You're good enough.'

Tania shook her head. 'I never really loved it. Not like skating. Ballet is good, but skating – it's like flying. No contest.'

Zac nodded. 'I know what you mean. That class this morning – it was good. Hard work, satisfying – but it's not like being on the ice.'

Tania smiled. 'I thought you just skated because you were having a laugh.'

'I do,' said Zac. 'Ice skating is hilarious. Really. I mean, think about it. A big frozen lake – indoors. Two thin strips of metal attached to the bottom of your shoes. And you go round and round, never actually getting anywhere. And the hardest things to do are the bits when your skates are meant to *leave* the ice – not skating at all!'

Tania couldn't help laughing. The way Zac described it made her dreams, fears and ambition all seem a bit daft – but in a good way. And he was right, after all – it was a strange thing to do, when you thought about it. 'You are an idiot.'

'Speaking of skates,' said Zac, 'I took mine in to be sharpened first thing this morning. To the same guy who does yours. Brock told me.'

'Good,' said Tania. 'That should help a bit. But I don't understand why you don't just buy a new pair. That pair is almost broken down completely. They're getting dangerous. You could break an ankle.'

'As long as I don't break yours.' Zac winked.

'You won't,' said Tania.

'Not on purpose . . .' said Zac. Tania looked at him with a frown, but then realized he was joking again.

'Why do you *do* that?' she asked in exasperation.

'Do what?'

'Say something you don't mean, to wind me up.'

Zac's expression dropped. 'It was just a joke, Tania.'

'Well, it wasn't very funny,' muttered Tania.

They ate in silence for a few moments. Then Zac sighed. 'Why won't you tell me?'

'Tell you what?'

'What's really bothering you. What this is all about.'

She looked up in alarm. 'What do you mean?'

'Come on, Tania.' He leaned forward and gazed at her. 'I know there's something, some major thing that happened, that's making you scared on the ice. People as good as you don't just stop being good. You don't get scared out of nowhere.'

Tania poked miserably at her chips. 'I can't. It's stupid.'

'It can't be stupid if it's making you so scared.' Zac's voice softened. 'I'm your partner. I know we haven't been skating together that long, but you need to trust me.'

She bit her lip. He sounded so kind, and she was sure he meant it. But she'd carried around this secret fear for so many months now, it was hard to think about letting it out. Tania looked into Zac's face and said, 'You're right. There was something, something that happened. Not to me – to someone else. It's changed everything for me.' She hesitated. 'I will tell you. I just – not now. OK?'

He nodded, though she could tell he was disappointed. 'We should probably get back to the rehearsal anyway, shouldn't we?'

♥

Tania was relieved when they were told sternly that no talking would be permitted in the auditorium. She had a lot of thinking to do. *It's time to open up*, she told herself sternly. *He's been nothing but kind and supportive, why can't you just blurt it all out? And besides, just because it happened to Kerri doesn't mean it will happen to you. It was an accident, pure and simple. It's just that it's played on your mind so much . . .*

Zac will understand. Won't he? Tania stared at the stage, though her mind was churning.

The two of them sat silently on the comfortable red seats of the Apollo auditorium and watched the rehearsal begin. It was a new piece, based on the folk tale of *Hansel and Gretel*, but with a twist. The two children were shown to be spoilt and unlikeable, taking advantage of an old woman who lived in the forest alone.

Tania began to relax as the rehearsal went on. There were moments when the company director would stop the dancers, take them back over something, call up to the lighting box, or shout for a stage manager. But there were only two days to go before opening night, so the show was almost ready.

'I didn't realize there was so much technical stuff,' Zac leaned over to whisper in Tania's ear. 'Is theatre always this complicated?'

'I guess so. Haven't you been to the theatre before?'

'Once,' said Zac, shrugging. 'A pantomime when I was little.'

Tania stared at him. 'Only once?'

'Quiet over there!' The director cast an irritated glance in their direction. Tania and Zac mumbled apologies and sank into silence again. Tania tried to concentrate on what was happening on stage, but her mind was humming. It didn't help that Zac's arm was almost touching hers, and she could feel the warmth radiating off him. *Just tell him! He's nice – he'll understand. And he said such sweet things about you to Suki, and he didn't mind you hearing, either. He's on your side!*

Besides, Tania suddenly realized, *if you don't tell him, you'll never be able to work with him as Brock intended. You'll never be proper partners if you keep secrets like that from each other. And so far, Zac has been completely honest with you, hasn't he? You owe it to him. And yourself. It's time to face up to what happened.*

Tania felt a swirling in her stomach, like the nervous excitement she got before a performance or a skating exam. *I'm going to tell him! As soon as we get out of here!* She drummed her fingers on the arm of the chair.

'Take twenty everyone!' called the director a little later, and Tania turned to Zac, her insides a whirlpool of anticipation.

'You want to get some air?'

Zac nodded gratefully. 'And stretch my legs. I'm stiffening up after that class this morning.'

They made their way outside and took big gulps of air. 'Is the sun still out?' said Tania, feeling surprised. 'Inside, it could be any time.'

Zac looked at his watch. 'It's only three. We don't have to stay for the rest of the rehearsal, though. I'm sure they wouldn't mind.'

'Brock wanted us to stay.'

'He did, but surely the point was to show me how important the little details are,' said Zac. 'I get it. Really I do.' He looked at Tania. 'Unless you want to stay to see the end?'

Tania didn't have to think twice. 'No, I'm OK. It's a good show though.' *I hope*, she thought. *I didn't really pay much attention because I was so busy thinking about other things.*

'Yeah. And that routine we learned this morning looks so much cooler when they do it.'

They went in to thank the director, who barely batted an eyelid, and then they were back outside with their bags. 'You want to get a coffee or something?' said Zac, just as Tania said, 'Do you have to go right now?'

They looked at each other and smiled. 'You can spare the time?' teased Zac. 'I mean, you haven't got homework or anything like that?'

'You're the one who took time off college to skate all day,' Tania retorted. 'Don't *you* have work to do?'

Zac laughed. '*Touché*. I guess you have a sense of humour after all.'

Tania was about to flare up in response when she saw the look in his eye. 'You won't get me again.'

His face lit up in delight. 'See? Not so easy to wind up now.'

They set off down the road. 'I have something to tell you,' Tania said, as though the words were bursting out of her.

Zac glanced at her sideways, one eyebrow raised, but he merely said, 'Wait till we've got drinks.'

Once settled at a café on the corner of the street, Zac looked expectantly at Tania. 'So?'

'You were right all the time,' she burst out. 'It was something that happened. About six months ago. On the ice.'

Zac nodded, his eyes fixed on her face. 'Go on.'

'It was my friend Kerri.' Tania's fingers gripped her orange juice. 'She fell. Doing a jump. The triple axel.'

Zac nodded again.

Tania ploughed on, the words tumbling out of her now she had started. 'We were training at the same time – I was literally about five metres away when she fell. There was this awful sound.' She swallowed. 'A really loud crack, it kind of echoed around the rink. And I looked over at Kerri and she was lying on the ice, with her leg bent out at a funny angle. Her face . . . it was the same colour as the ice. She just looked at me. And then she passed out.'

'Wow.'

'She broke her leg in five places,' Tania said, and her voice shook slightly. 'Her career was over. And the funny thing was, *we both knew it*. When she looked at me, before she fainted – *we both knew*. That was it. In one second, everything over.'

Zac sipped his coffee. 'That's scary,' he observed in a calm tone. 'Watching that. And knowing how bad it must be.'

'But that's not the worst bit.' Tania bit her lip again. Now that she had come to it, she wasn't sure she could admit it – the worst part, the part that kept her awake at night and brought the guilt crashing down on her. 'Kerri was the top junior skater at the rink. I was always second to her.' She looked down at her fingers. They were clenched so tightly round the glass of juice that they were white as the tablecloth.

Zac waited.

'I was glad,' whispered Tania. 'When she fell. And when she looked at me, she knew what I was thinking.'

'You thought you could be number one now,' Zac said softly.

'Yes.' Tania's eyes suddenly filled with tears and her

throat burned. 'I feel so guilty. And I think maybe that's why I can't do it any more. Because I was glad it wasn't me, you know? I was glad it was her who fell and not me – and now I can't stop thinking about it and panicking that the same thing will happen to me. Because I deserve it.'

'But it wasn't *your* fault.'

'No, but that's not the point. I shouldn't have looked at her that way. My first thought should have been for *her*. But all I could think about was *me*, and how her bad luck was my good luck.' She wiped her eyes hastily.

Zac tactfully looked away. 'I can see why it might have been getting to you.'

'It's ridiculous,' Tania said more firmly, as though trying to convince herself. 'It was months ago now, and it's not even as if I see Kerri any more. She moved up north somewhere to get physio at a special hospital.' Her breath caught in her throat but she steadied herself. 'It's just that every time I prepare for a jump, I hear that awful noise in my head – that crack of her leg breaking – and I just know I'm going to mess up again.'

'Why haven't you talked to Brock about it? I'm sure he could help.'

Tania shook her head violently. 'I can't. He was

Kerri's coach too. I can't admit . . . that I was glad.'

'But you're not glad now, are you?' Zac looked up, frowning. 'Are you?'

'I don't know!' Tania felt like wailing. 'If Kerri had carried on skating, she'd still be better than me. I'd still be second best. Of *course* I didn't want her to break her leg, to lose her career, all her hopes and dreams . . . but at the same time, it means *I'm* at the top spot now.' She stopped. 'You think I'm heartless.' *This was such a dreadful mistake. I shouldn't have told him. Why would he want to skate with me now that he knows what sort of a person I really am?*

'Tania,' said Zac, 'you've got to stop blaming yourself. You're ambitious. You've been trained to think you're the best. You've been taught to put winning above everything else. I can see why you'd have that reaction.' He hesitated. 'Have you kept in touch with Kerri?'

'She didn't want to. I think she was angry with me. Angry that it happened to her, I mean, and not to someone else.' Tania wiped her eyes again. 'I can understand that. I did try to talk to her; I went round a couple of times after she came home from hospital. But then her mum started saying Kerri didn't want visitors, and I knew it was just me.'

'She didn't want to see you because you reminded her of what she'd lost.'

'Exactly.'

Zac let out his breath very slowly. 'Wow.' They sat in silence for a moment. Then he said, 'Thank you for telling me.'

Tania nodded. 'I'll talk to Brock on Monday and say it's not working out. You needn't worry, I'll sort it out.'

He stared at her. 'What do you mean?'

'Well, you don't want to skate with me any more, do you?' Tania concentrated hard on her fingers. If she looked up, she'd see his expression, and she wasn't sure she could cope with it. 'I mean, after what I've just told you . . . you must think . . .'

'Stop telling me what I think,' Zac interrupted. He sounded frustrated. 'The trouble with *you*, Tania, is that you think everything's about you. So you feel guilty, fair enough. You're scared of the triple axel because it ruined Kerri's career and it could easily have been you. I get that. But this is meant to be about *us* – you and me skating together. If you'd confessed to me that you'd pushed Kerri over and she'd broken her leg, then I might have thought twice about skating with you. But this is something that happened to someone else, and you couldn't have done anything about it. What we have to do now is figure out how to move on.'

'I've been trying to do that since it happened,' said Tania, irritated.

Zac gave her a sudden grin. 'Yes, but you didn't have *me* around to help, did you?' A thought struck him. 'Besides, tomorrow will be a good challenge.'

'Tomorrow?'

'Yeah.' The grin grew wider. 'SkyJumpers, remember? If anything can help you overcome a fear of falling, that will.'

Tania's eyes were big with shock. All of the confused and messed-up feelings suddenly congealed into a frozen block of fear. SkyJumpers! How could she have forgotten!

Chapter 11

i'm full of surprises

Tania didn't sleep at all well. For one thing, she was nervous about the next day. High wires and rope bridges! It all sounded like her worst nightmare. At two o'clock in the morning, she wondered if she could call Brock and pretend she'd come down with the flu. But even if he believed her (which was unlikely), he'd probably just make her go another day.

But it wasn't just the thought of SkyJumpers that was keeping her awake. The conversation with Zac re-played over and over again in her mind. She couldn't believe she'd told him about Kerri's accident. She hadn't told *anyone* how she felt; not her mother, not Brock, not Libby . . . but she had told Zac. Why him? Was she, perhaps, finally beginning to trust him? Did that mean she could let go more on the ice as well as off? She thought about his reaction again: he'd been firmly reassuring.

It wasn't your fault, he'd said. *It's time to move on.*

In some ways, it was a huge relief to have admitted her fears. Zac hadn't laughed at her; hadn't told her she was being stupid. He'd understood why such a terrible accident had had such an effect on her own skating. Why she was now frightened of the big jumps, especially the triple axel. He'd said they were in it together: *we*, he said. *We need to figure out how to move forward*. The word gave her a warm feeling.

But that was the new scary part, wasn't it? Because Tania was becoming aware that she didn't think of Zac as just her skating partner any more. There were other, newer, complicated feelings swimming around, bobbing their heads to the surface and making her nervous. It was a big thing to admit to herself. Tania had never had a boyfriend. She'd always told Libby it was because she didn't have time for one, and that was partly true. Skating took up so much of her life, there was barely time for school, let alone a boyfriend. But maybe there was a small part of her that had always been nervous around boys. There were boys at school, but when all the other girls had been hanging out round the bike sheds and giggling about them, Tania had been hanging out at the rink and working hard at her skating. When Libby had had her first kiss and told Tania about it in graphic detail, Tania had listened as though from another world.

And now she had admitted her secret fear to the boy who . . . well, she maybe liked a bit more than as a friend. She had made herself vulnerable to someone she was starting to care about. Had she been right to pull down that barrier? Barriers were good, they helped protect your feelings and made you strong. Opening up to Zac . . . would it make her weak? What if . . . what if she opened up too much and he just walked away?

Tania rubbed her face in her pillow. Up to now, her life had been so straightforward – skating and school. But now that Zac was here, things had suddenly got so much more confusing.

♥

'You OK?' asked Zac. 'You look really tired.'

'I'm fine,' said Tania, trying not to yawn. 'Just didn't sleep well.'

Zac nodded sympathetically. 'Don't worry about it. You'll be fine.'

Tania gave a weak smile. *It's OK, he thinks you're just nervous about today. Which you are, so that's kind of true.*

The minibus took them to Whitstable Wood, which was only a twenty-minute journey. There were six other young people on board, all of whom were SkyJumper regulars and who spent the whole journey talking about their favourite activities. By the time they arrived, Tania felt more nervous than ever. It didn't help that Zac had become more and more excited by what he had heard. 'I hope we get to try the ten-metre zip-wire!' he enthused. Tania closed her eyes briefly and tried not to think about it.

On arrival, the six regulars peeled off and disappeared into the woods. Tania and Zac headed to the reception area, where a stocky bloke called Pete took their details and asked them to fill in some health and safety forms. The two of them dutifully ticked all the 'no' boxes on the sheets and handed them back.

Pete grinned. 'Excellent. Looks like you're both in tip-top condition. You can join the first lot over there for the safety film.'

Tania and Zac joined a small group of young people, some of whom (Tania was pleased to notice) looked as nervous as she did. Zac was jiggling up and down, impatient to get going. Tania just felt sick.

Pete came to show them a short film and gave them a talk on safety harnesses and hand signals. 'There's no shame in asking for help,' he said cheerfully. 'We'd rather you asked for help than tried to do something you're not happy with. On the other hand,' he grinned, 'our motto here is "if you don't leap, you can't fly" and if you try not to worry too much, you might surprise yourselves.'

'Yeah, right,' muttered Tania. Her hands felt cold and clammy.

'Remember,' Pete added. 'Everything here is completely safe. We won't let you fall. Besides, if you die, we'll get closed down!' He roared with laughter.

'I don't think that was very funny,' said Tania, annoyed that Zac was chuckling.

'Lighten up, Tania,' said Zac. 'You'll be fine.' He put an arm around her shoulders and gave her a brief hug, but Tania was too tense to feel anything but cold fear.

Pete led the group out to their first obstacle – a five-metre-high climbing net. Tania stared up at it.

'Right, first four into your harnesses,' said Pete. Zac leaped forward, but when he saw Tania hanging back, he reluctantly joined her.

'We'll watch the first lot, OK?' he said. Tania nodded.

The volunteers were clipped into harnesses, and

one strong-looking man held the end of each rope. 'We take your weight,' Pete told them. 'So if you slip or fall, you won't drop more than a couple of feet. We'll make sure of that.'

Tania and Zac watched the climbers start up the net. Two of them made good headway, though the other two were slower. 'The net moves about so much,' said Tania.

Pete heard her. 'It's anchored at the ends and the sides, but you're right, it does wave a bit. You need to concentrate on where you're putting hands and feet. Like climbing a wall in a strong wind.' He looked at Tania. 'Though I'm guessing you haven't done that either.' She shook her head. Pete grinned. 'Don't worry,' he said. 'It won't be as bad as you think.'

Before Tania knew it, the first four were over the top of the net and coming down the other side. Not one of them had needed help from their harness. Pete nodded at her. 'Up you go then.'

Tania glanced at Zac. His eyes were shining. 'Come on, then,' he said.

Tania stood very still as she was clipped into her harness. *If I don't think about it*, she thought, *then it might be easier. Don't look up. Don't look down. Concentrate on one hand, one foot – one step at a time. Whatever you do, don't think about falling.*

Zac was already halfway up the net before Tania had even taken three steps. Hands shaking, she started up. One hand up. The other hand. One foot. The other foot.

Rather to her surprise, it wasn't as hard as she'd feared. Her natural sense of balance kept her from swinging about too much, and she almost enjoyed the challenge of finding a suitable hand- or foot-hold. Before she knew it, Tania had reached the huge wooden beam at the top. Zac was sitting astride it, beaming at her. 'There you go! Told you it would be OK!'

Tania gave him a shaky smile. 'Not too bad,' she said, trying to sound casual.

Zac laughed. 'Over you come then, and after that it's easy.'

'Over . . .' Tania put her hands on the beam, and the net suddenly swung alarmingly. Panicked, she gripped hard and pulled herself close to the beam. The world swayed around her, and she couldn't help looking down. At once, the ground seemed to rush up to meet her, and her ears echoed with that sickening crack again. She squeezed her eyes shut.

'You'll never get over like that,' said Zac. 'You need to swing one leg over then the other.'

'Yes, in a minute,' snapped Tania, her heart racing. *Move your leg*, she told herself. But nothing happened.

Her whole body was rigid. It was as though it had completely turned to stone.

'Tania?' said Zac. His voice changed tone. 'You OK?'

She couldn't answer him; couldn't even look at him. She heard him moving towards her, along the beam. Then his voice was close in her ear. 'Tania, it's me, Zac. You're thinking about that accident again, aren't you?'

Eyes still firmly shut, she nodded.

Zac's voice was quiet and gentle. 'It's OK, Tania. You're not going to fall. I'm going to help you.'

'Everything all right up there?' Tania heard Pete's distant voice.

'Just give us a minute,' Zac shouted back.

'Tell her to let go,' shouted Pete. 'We'll lower her to the ground.'

Tania found herself shaking her head furiously.

'We'll be OK,' called Zac. 'Just give us a second.' He bent towards Tania again. 'You can let go, you know. It'll be OK. They'll make sure you get down safely.'

Tania was still shaking her head. 'Can't,' she muttered.

'What?'

'Can't.' Tania felt as though her teeth were welded together with fear. 'Can't move my arms.'

'OK. Then we're going to do this really slowly. Open your eyes, Tania. Look at me.'

Slowly Tania lifted her head. Her neck creaked with

the effort. She met Zac's eyes. They were shining with encouragement, and somehow, something inside her relaxed slightly. Zac nodded. 'You can do this.' He put his hand over hers. It was as though the warmth from him was gradually transferring itself into her own hand. The icy panic started to thaw. Tania twitched her fingers. 'That's good,' said Zac. 'Now lift your hand off the beam. I won't let you fall.'

It felt like an eternity, but slowly, slowly, Zac talked Tania over the top of the beam. Two more people came up and over the net in that time, but Zac ignored them. Patiently, keeping his voice low, he talked to Tania as though she were a small child. 'That's good, that's really good. Well done. Now you just have to move that foot a little bit to your left. Great.'

Moving a little faster now they were over the net, Tania and Zac climbed down the other side. Tania's breath was coming in little gasps, but she no longer felt like she was going to pass out. Zac kept pace with her all the time, even though she knew he must be itching to race down and get to the next thing. Finally she felt solid ground under her foot, and the breath whooshed out of her.

Pete was looking at her. 'You OK? Tania, isn't it?'

She nodded. 'Yes. I'm OK.' Though actually she felt like bursting into tears with the relief.

Pete clapped Zac on the back. 'Excellent work up there. If you ever want a job here, let me know. We can train you up.'

Zac's eyes nearly fell out of his head. 'Really? Wow, thanks.'

'So,' said Pete, 'if everyone's OK, we'll move on to the next thing.'

Zac hung back for a moment to speak to Tania. 'How are you feeling now?'

She looked up at him, and for a moment she couldn't speak. Through all her panic and fear, he had been a constant reassurance. He hadn't let her fall. She felt as though her whole heart and being was pouring out towards him. He took a step backwards, as though rocked by some unseen force. 'Thank you,' she said. 'I can't begin to tell you . . . thank you.'

'That's OK,' he said, and cleared his throat. His cheeks coloured slightly. 'That's OK,' he said more firmly. 'Any time.' He held out his hand, and together they walked to the next task.

♥

As the day wore on, Tania felt as though something inside her was changing. The block of immobilizing icy fear was beginning to melt. After that first task, each successive obstacle had seemed slightly easier. She still felt that moment of panic as she stood at the beginning of a rope bridge, or at the top of a wall, but it was no longer paralysing her in the same way. She had even managed to smile whilst abseiling.

'Right,' said Pete. 'This is it. The big one.'

It was an enormous zip-wire, perhaps ten metres up in the air. A large platform was secured between several trees. The thin wire stretched from the platform to the ground – at least, Tania assumed it did, since she couldn't actually see the end of it from the platform. She could feel Zac glance at her.

'This is the last activity you'll do today,' said Pete, 'and it's the best by far. You don't have to do anything at all – just step off the platform and fly down to the ground. If you have the chance, look around you as you go, because it's a great view over the countryside.'

'How many goes can we have?' Zac asked, excitement in his voice.

Pete laughed. 'Just the one, Zac. Sorry, no time for more. So make it count.'

'Tania?' said Zac in a low voice. 'Do you want to do this?'

She turned to him. *It's funny*, she thought to herself, *but when I'm standing next to Zac, I feel as though I can do anything*. 'Of course,' she said.

Zac looked surprised but pleased. He grinned. 'Good for you. You want to go first?'

'No, it's OK,' she told him. 'You go. I'll see you at the bottom.'

'Zac, you volunteering?' Pete called over.

Zac shook his head. 'What if you freeze up again? I'll wait until you've gone.'

'No.' Tania was firm. 'I won't freeze. Honestly. Please. Let me do it on my own.'

'Zac?' said Pete.

'OK.' Zac gave her a long look. 'I'll see you down there.'

Within seconds, Zac was clipped into the harness, shown how to hold his arms, given a countdown, and launched into space. Tania watched him speed off into the trees, his yell of delight making everyone below look up.

'Tania, you going next?' asked Pete.

'No,' said Tania. 'Let the others go.'

'Sure? Don't put it off.'

'I'm not.' Tania smiled at him. 'It's OK, Pete. I'm just – you know. Chilling out.' *Taking a moment. Preparing myself. Zac can't hold my hand on this one, but I know he's still here, in my head, telling me it'll be all right.*

Pete laughed. 'Right you are. OK then, who's up next?'

One by one, the rest of the group took off into space, the air punctuated with squeals and shouts. Finally there was only Tania left.

'Come on then,' said Pete, holding out the harness. 'Time to go.'

Tania felt as though her body had gone into some kind of freefall even before she was harnessed up. Her mind seemed to be floating above her, looking down with interest as her body made its preparations. Zac's face swam into her mind. An eerie feeling of calmness spread through her.

'Three, two, one – *go*,' said Pete, and Tania stepped off the platform.

The speed was immediate. The wind rushed through her hair and made her blink. The sound of the zip-wire was loud in her ears, but just at that moment, a shaft of sunlight jutted into her path, and Tania slid straight into it. The sudden warmth on her face made her open her eyes, and she felt her breath taken away by the view. Below her, the trees dropped away suddenly, and there was a split-second glimpse of rolling green hills and waving grasses. Then the light was dimmed again as she plunged down between the trees.

It was extraordinary. Could it be any closer to flying? And it reminded her of something . . . but what was it? Tania's face broke into a smile. It reminded her of *skating*. On an impulse, she flung her arms wide and laughed. The movement sent her swinging, and for a second adrenalin flooded her body, but it was a good panic – a come-alive fear – a shot of danger. She pulled in her arms as the ground approached, and placed her feet squarely on the path, knees bent to absorb the impact.

'Nice landing,' the instructor at the bottom said admiringly. 'You've got a good sense of balance.'

'I'm a skater,' said Tania as he unclipped her from the harness and helped her out. Warmth spread through her at the words. 'I'm a skater,' she repeated proudly.

'You certainly are,' said Zac, who had been watching from the side. 'I thought you weren't going to come down.'

Tania smiled at him. 'I had to. To prove something to myself.'

'So how was it?'

Tania paused for a moment. 'Amazing. Really amazing.'

'Wasn't it?' said Zac, his face breaking into an answering smile. 'I wish we could go again.'

'No,' said Tania. 'Once was enough. Once was perfect.'

Zac looked at her curiously. 'You look a bit – I dunno. Weirdly calm. Are you OK?'

No, she wanted to tell him, *I'm not OK, I'm more than OK, and it's because of you. You told me I could trust you, and now it's like part of me has remembered how to fly.* A small bubble of laughter popped into her throat as she wondered how he would react if she actually said any of that. 'I'm fine,' she said, trying to swallow down the laughter. 'Honestly, I'm fine.'

'You look great,' said Zac, and then looked away, his cheeks flushing with colour again. Tania barely noticed. 'I guess it's time to go home.'

'Yeah. Yes. And back to the rink.' As Tania said it she thought, *It's going to be OK now. I'm sure it is. I can fly again.*

Chapter 12

a thousand pounds

'So,' said Brock on Monday morning, 'how did it go?'

Tania glanced at Zac. 'Good. Really good.'

Zac nodded. 'I think we both had some kind of breakthrough.'

And how! thought Tania. She couldn't wait to get onto the ice. Her feet were practically itching with eagerness, the way they used to in the old days.

Brock looked searchingly from one to the other. 'Good. You don't have to tell me about it unless you want to. It's enough that you've talked to each other.' He rubbed his hands together. 'Right then, we'll see what sort of a difference it's made.' He put them through a gruelling warm-up and then moved straight on to the lifts.

Tania was not surprised to find she was far more relaxed about letting Zac lift her. The way he had talked her over the rope net; the conversations they had had on the Saturday – everything felt easier now that she had decided to trust him. Kerri's accident was still there, at the back of her head, but it felt smaller somehow, as if it were further away.

Zac too noticed the difference. 'You're so easy to lift today,' he told her. 'It's like you're made of air.'

Encouraged by their progress, Brock called them over and asked for the death spiral. 'Just take it easy,' he said to Tania, who nodded.

'I know. It'll be OK now, I think.'

And it was. The first one was a little shaky, but each time after that was better. After the fourth spiral, Brock clapped his hands. 'Good! You're getting there! Well done!'

Tania and Zac grinned at each other. 'He doesn't say that often,' whispered Zac.

'I know,' Tania replied in a low voice. 'We should record it so we can play it back whenever we like.'

'No chatting!' called Brock. 'Work to do!'

Zac reached for Tania's hand as they skated over for the next instruction. His hand was warm and reassuring, just as it had been on the rope net. Tania felt another chunk of ice melt away.

At the end of the session, Brock called them both to the barrier. 'Some very good work today, both of you,' he said. 'The weekend seems to have knocked some sense into you. Tania, you're much more relaxed, and it's showing in the quality of your edges. Zac, your core strength is better, and having your skates sharpened properly has made a big difference.' He frowned. 'Though you still really need new skates. It's a priority now. You can't partner Tania in the show without decent skates – and you need time to break them in too. We've only got a month left.'

Zac looked down at the ice. 'Yeah, well . . .'

'Is it the money, Zac?' Brock asked, his voice surprisingly gentle. 'Skates are expensive.'

Zac shrugged. 'I guess.'

Tania tried to look as though she wasn't listening. She fiddled with the laces on her boots.

'Can't your parents help out?' asked Brock.

'Not really,' mumbled Zac. 'They don't have much money.'

'What about a part-time job?'

'I have one,' said Zac shortly. 'I work for Mum and Dad.'

Tania raised her eyebrows but said nothing. What did his parents do? Why had she never asked him about his home life? *Because I was too busy being selfish and obsessed with my own problems*, she realized.

'I get paid,' said Zac, 'but it all goes on skating already.'

Brock sighed. 'Well, we'll have to think of something. You can't go on like this. Your skates are holding you back.'

'Maybe I could get another second-hand pair . . . ?' suggested Zac hopefully.

Brock gave him a long look, and then slapped his hand on the barrier. 'Let's not think about it now. Good work today, both of you.' He grinned. 'I'm glad to see my little idea has worked out well. And tomorrow I'll tell you what you're skating to.'

The music! Any other time, Tania would have been itching to know what Brock had picked to accompany their programme. The music was almost the most important part of a skating programme, and usually Tania was keen to make her own suggestions. But this time she was far too busy thinking about Zac and his lack of money.

'What do your parents do?' she asked as they headed back to the lockers.

'They run a pub.'

'A pub?' Tania felt surprised. 'Really?'

'Yeah, why?' He stopped.

'Oh, nothing,' Tania said hastily. She didn't want him to think she was being snobby. 'That must be hard work.'

'Yeah, it is. Thirteen-hour days and they never go

on holiday. They even work Christmas and bank holidays.' He shrugged. 'But they like the customers. Most of them, that is.'

'So what do you do when you work for them?'

'Washing up, carrying food to tables, cleaning – that kind of thing.' He looked at her sharply. 'I won't be doing it for ever.'

'I wasn't suggesting . . .'

'I'm going to go to university,' Zac went on, a determined edge to his voice. 'I don't want to work in a pub all my life. I'm going to get good grades from college and study engineering. I'll be the first in my family to graduate. My older brother went to uni but he dropped out after one term.'

'Engineering?'

'Yeah. I'm studying maths, physics and psychology at the moment.'

Tania couldn't help the look on her face.

'You don't have to look so surprised,' Zac commented. 'What did you think I was doing? Some vocational diploma in car maintenance?'

'No, of course not . . .' Tania glanced at the floor in confusion. 'Sorry. I didn't realize.'

He took a breath. 'Don't worry about it. Sorry, I probably over-reacted there a bit. It's just . . . I look at my parents and see how hard they work for so little, and I know I don't want that for myself. I want more prospects, more options.'

'What about skating? Isn't that an option?'

Zac let out a laugh and his whole body relaxed. 'Only you would ask that.'

'Well, isn't it?' Tania was puzzled. 'You could earn good money, you know. Competing.'

'It's not much of a life though, is it?' said Zac. 'Always working on the same tricks, travelling everywhere for the competitions. And on the day, it just comes down to who lands their triple lutz. A whole career-defining moment comes down to one jump.'

'But that's the excitement of it,' said Tania. 'That's the adrenalin. That's what pushes you to keep going, to get better – the thought that one day it will all come together, be perfect.'

He smiled at her. 'You know, when you talk like that about it, I could almost be persuaded.' His face fell. 'Except for the start-up costs. I don't have those kinds of savings.'

Tania didn't know what to say.

Zac grinned again. 'Hey, it's OK. I'm enjoying it for now anyway. Skating with you is much more fun than messing around on my own.' He gave her a wave. 'See you tomorrow.'

'Yeah.'

Tania went home in a thoughtful mood. She'd always had money. It wasn't that she was materialistic; it had just always been there. If she needed new skates, she told her parents, who bought them for her. If she needed more ballet lessons or more time at the rink – all of that cost money, but Tania never really thought about it. It just happened by itself.

♥

'Mum,' said Tania, once they were home, 'how much have I cost you over the years?'

Caroline grinned. 'Do you mean my money or my sanity?'

Tania gave a half-laugh. 'The money. How much money have you paid for me to keep skating?'

Her mother's brow creased. 'I don't know. Why?'

'Hundreds?' pressed Tania. 'Thousands?'

'Thousands, certainly,' said Caroline. 'A lot, I suppose, if you added it up over the years. Your skates cost over a thousand pounds on their own, and every time your feet grow, you need a new pair.'

Tania nodded. 'And then there's ballet and I suppose Brock costs money too.'

'He certainly does,' said Caroline, rolling her eyes. 'A very expensive coach, especially for individual lessons.

But he's the best, or so they said. And he's been good for you.'

'I wonder how Zac manages to pay him then?' mused Tania.

Caroline turned to look at her daughter. 'Zac? What sort of family does he come from?'

'He said his parents didn't go to university and now they run a pub.'

'Run a pub? Wow, that's hard work. I wouldn't want to do that.'

'But somehow they must pay for him to skate, mustn't they?' asked Tania, frowning. 'I mean, surely his part-time wages wouldn't pay for Brock?'

Caroline filled the kettle and switched it on. 'Cup of tea? I don't know how they do it, Tania, but I do know one thing. When you're a parent, you want the best for your child. If that means going without something for yourself so that your child can have something they need, then you just do it.'

'Like what?'

'Well.' Caroline pulled up a chair and sat down as the kettle started hissing. 'Remember last year when you went to that competition in Sweden?'

'Yes.' Tania screwed up her nose. 'I messed up the double salchow.'

'You got silver. That was excellent.'

'Not gold, though.'

'Anyway,' said Caroline, 'your father and I had booked to go away that week. It was our twentieth wedding anniversary, remember?'

'Um . . .'

'It's all right. I don't expect you to remember things like that. We had a nice dinner out instead. But we had to cancel our week away so that we could take you to Sweden.'

Tania stared. 'You never told me that.'

Caroline shrugged. 'What for? I didn't want you to feel guilty about it. We made the choice. We could have told you that Sweden was impossible. But you really wanted to compete, so we just cancelled the holiday. We'll go another time.'

'But it was your twentieth wedding anniversary!'

'Then maybe we'll go for our twenty-fifth.' The kettle clicked off, and Caroline got up to make tea. 'The point is, Tania, that parents give up a lot for their children because they *want* to. And it's worth it too. We're so proud of you. And when you won silver in Sweden, it was worth us having given up our holiday. Watching you skate out there . . .' Caroline sighed. 'It was beautiful. You're so lucky, Tania, to be so talented.'

'I know.' Tania ran her thumb over the handle of

her mug. Memories rippled through her: of Sweden, winning the silver (not the gold! So close!); her mother driving her to the rink at six a.m., bleary-eyed; her father ringing to book flights to the various countries in which she would compete; spending time on the Internet, researching different sorts of skating blades . . .

But there had never been any question of money. 'Mum,' Tania began, 'what can I do about Zac? He needs new skates.'

Caroline looked at her daughter. 'New skates? Then . . . oh, I see.' She sat back and gazed at Tania thoughtfully. 'He can't afford them, right? And you were wondering . . .'

'It's a silly idea,' said Tania hastily. 'He's not your responsibility.'

'Or yours,' pointed out Caroline.

'Well, that's the thing,' said Tania. 'He kind of is, you know? He's my skating partner. And he's good, Mum. I think he could be really good, in time.' She squirmed as she said, 'I like skating with him. He makes me remember why I like skating so much. He's helping me get over my – my problems. I'm getting better again, Mum.'

Her mother raised her eyebrows. 'That's wonderful. I'm so glad it's working out after all.'

'I have some savings, don't I?' Tania stared at her mug of tea. 'Savings that are just mine, right?'

'Right.'

'And I can spend them on whatever I like?'

Caroline took a sip of tea. 'We were hoping you might keep the money for the future. You know, for a house or a car or something like that.'

'Can I take out a thousand pounds?' asked Tania.

'To buy Zac skates.'

Tania nodded. 'I'd like to do something in return.'

Caroline was silent for a moment. Then a smile spread across her face. 'You know, Tania, I think that's the first time I've heard you ask for something that isn't for yourself.'

Tania blushed. 'I know I haven't always been very . . . Well, maybe I haven't thought about others enough . . .'

Her mother rescued her. 'It's a very generous offer, you know. Very generous.'

'I want to do it for Zac,' mumbled Tania.

'I know, and I think it's extremely kind of you. Maybe Zac is good for you in other ways, not just your skating. And I am absolutely fine with it, if you're sure.'

'Really?' Tania looked up.

Caroline smiled. 'Really. It's a very grown-up thing

to do. And very unselfish. But, Tania, have you thought about it properly?'

'What do you mean?'

'You can't just *give* Zac all that money,' said Caroline gently.

'Why not?'

'Think about it from his point of view,' said Caroline. 'Think how he would feel. He has very little money; he works hard for the bit he's saved up. And here's this girl, younger than him, who's got enough money that she can just give away a thousand pounds! How would you feel?'

'Embarrassed,' said Tania. 'I see what you mean.'

'I don't think he would accept it from you,' said Caroline. 'He'd feel humiliated, and like he has to pay it back in some way.'

'But he doesn't.'

'I know that. It's a present. But a thousand pounds is a very big present, Tania. I think you're going to have to find some other way of giving him the money, so he doesn't know it's from you.'

'How can I do that?'

Caroline smiled again. 'I think you're going to have to be a little devious . . .'

Chapter 13

trying something new

'So is it tonight you get to hear your music?' asked Libby as they carried their bags back to the lockers.

Tania nodded. 'I love the moment I first hear it on the ice. As long as it's good, that is. But Brock usually picks good stuff.'

'I bet it'll be something really romantic,' said Libby, stuffing her English folder into her over-full locker.

'You'll never get that folder in.'

'Yes, I will.' Libby shoved, and the spine of the folder cracked, spilling paper all over the floor. 'Rats.'

'Besides, you need that folder for homework. We've got that essay on *Jane Eyre*, remember?'

Libby made a noise of annoyance. 'Couldn't you have said that five seconds earlier? Before I broke it?'

Tania laughed. 'It's not my fault you have the memory of a goldfish.' She opened her own, tidily organized locker. 'If you lined things up neatly, you'd get more in.'

'I'm not tidy, you know that.'

'I know.' Tania grinned. 'Besides, you were thinking about Scott Fanshawe.'

Libby's jaw dropped. 'How did you know that?'

Tania rolled her eyes. 'Come on, Lib, I'm your best friend, remember? It's so obvious!'

'God, is it?' Libby ran her hand through her hair distractedly. 'He hasn't noticed, has he?'

'Libby, the whole class has noticed.' Tania slammed her locker shut and turned the key. 'But you once told me that boys never notice these things, so maybe you've got away with it.' Her eyes strayed across the hall for a moment.

Libby looked at her closely. 'You were just thinking about Zac, weren't you?'

'No,' Tania mumbled.

'Ha!' Libby leaned hard against her locker to get the door to shut. 'Does he know you fancy him?'

'I don't.'

Libby turned to face her friend and sighed. 'Tania, it's OK to like a boy, you know. Why can't you just admit it? You get this funny look on your face now when you talk about him. You even say his name differently than you used to. And I caught you doodling his name on your chemistry book earlier.'

Tania blushed hotly. 'I did not.'

'You used your ink eradicator on it afterwards,' said Libby. 'I saw you.'

Tania sagged. 'All right. I don't know what's happening. I can't stop thinking about him. It's driving me crazy.'

'You're falling for him,' said Libby in a matter-of-fact way.

'But I can't do that!' Tania protested. 'He's my skating partner! It would be the worst thing ever.'

'Why?' asked Libby. The two of them started down the corridor. 'I mean, isn't there that Russian ice-skating couple? They're married, aren't they?'

'Yes . . .' said Tania reluctantly.

'And there's Melanie and the droolsome Fred from *Dancing On Ice*.' Libby turned to look at her. 'Honestly, what would be so bad?'

'What if he doesn't feel the same way?' said Tania. 'Or, even worse, what if he does feel the same way, and we start going out, and then we split up?'

Libby laughed. 'You are so funny. Can't you just concentrate on here and now? Besides . . .' She frowned. 'I thought you were only skating with Zac for this term? For the show. After that, you won't be partners any more, will you? So it doesn't matter, does it? I mean, it's not as though it would affect your skating.'

Tania opened her mouth to reply, but the words didn't come. Her heart had suddenly given an awful lurch. *After that, you won't be partners any more, will you?* She had spent so much time with Zac recently that going back to skating alone seemed like another world.

'You got time for a walk down the corner shop?' asked Libby. 'I need chocolate.'

'Sorry,' said Tania. 'Got to get to the rink.'

Libby blew out her cheeks. 'All right. I'll come with you.'

'What?'

'I think it's about time I saw this Zac in action, don't you?' Libby put her head on one side. 'No, don't argue. If you're going all doolally over him, I'm going to have to check him out, aren't I? How else can I help you with your boy issues?'

♥

'Right,' said Brock, 'are you ready?'

Tania glanced across the ice to where Libby was sitting on a side bench.

'Your friend isn't going to distract you, I hope,' said Brock, frowning.

Libby waved enthusiastically, and Tania quickly looked away, embarrassed. 'No, of course not.'

Zac opened his mouth to say something and then closed it again. *Does he know Libby's only come to watch so she can see what he's like?* Tania thought frantically. *No, he can't know. But what would he say if he knew? Even worse, what would he say if he knew how I was feeling about him?*

'This music,' said Zac, 'it'd better not be something slushy.'

Brock grinned and hit 'play'.

The introduction was bright and upbeat, and Tania frowned. She knew she'd heard it somewhere before. 'Is this George Michael?' said Zac.

'Good guess,' said Brock, as the song started. 'Duetting with Aretha Franklin. Have a listen.'

Tania leaned against the barrier and looked out across the ice. She grinned when she heard the chorus. 'Are you trying to tell us something, Brock?'

'Who, me?' said Brock innocently. 'What, like keeping going when things look bad? When the mountain was high, you still believed?'

Zac was tapping his foot. 'It's good. Nice easy rhythm, not too manic.'

'Or sloppy,' suggested Tania.

'Yeah.'

'What's it called?' asked Tania.

'"I Knew You Were Waiting",' said Zac immediately. 'My mum's got it on an album somewhere.'

'I like it,' said Tania. 'I think it's a grower.' Out of the corner of her eye, she could see Libby dancing along whilst still sitting on her bench. She gave Tania the thumbs up.

'Good,' said Brock. 'Then get out there on the ice and show me what you can do.'

'Huh?'

But Zac was already off, skimming his way around the rink. 'I think we should do some leaps,' he shouted. 'Sort of like this . . .'

Tania's jaw dropped. 'What was *that*?'

'Side-split leap,' said Brock calmly.

'I don't normally do things like that.'

Brock shrugged. 'So? This partnership is all about trying something new.'

Tania turned to face him, curious. 'And you don't normally ask for suggestions.'

Brock met her gaze. 'Zac's good at choreography,' he said simply. 'Inventive – original. He may not have had the years of training you have, but he's got lateral thinking.'

'It's not really a skating move,' yelled Zac, using his hand to spin him from one foot to the other, 'more of a skateboarding thing. But it might work on the ice.'

Tania shook her head in amazement. Skateboarding! On ice! But, she had to admit, that move did look kind of cool. 'How do you do that?' she called, skating over.

'OK, watch the left hand,' said Zac, and he demonstrated again. Libby cheered from her bench, and then clapped her hand over her mouth. Zac grinned at her.

It was a fun afternoon. Zac fell over more times than he could count. Tania laughed more than she had in weeks. Brock just watched and smiled. But amongst the joking around and the silly suggestions, a core of moves was growing and developing – moves far different from anything Tania had worked on before. Out went the straightforward crossovers and waltz jumps; in came cartwheels and double-swivelling stops. Libby went to the café at one point and bought muffins for everyone but was so fascinated by the session that she absent-mindedly ate them all, one after the other.

'Don't forget the potential of two bodies instead of one,' Brock said at one point, and immediately, Zac threw himself into designing spins for the two of them. Tania felt astonished at his originality – there seemed to be no end to his ideas. Of course, some of them didn't work; some of them were downright dangerous; but a few were pure genius. Tania felt a curious tingling in her stomach as she watched Zac try out a new spin. Every time she thought she'd got him figured out, he went and did something to surprise her. And he was talented too – how could she not have seen that to start with? Talent, brains and – yes – good looks. Almost too good to be true!

But he is real, Tania thought to herself. *And he's skating with me!* A hot flush crept over her cheeks.

Zac called over, 'Tania, you gotta try this. I can't do it on my own.' Tania heard Libby make an 'ooh' noise as she skated over, but ignored it.

She was wheezing with the effort when Brock finally called them over to finish. 'That's the hardest I've seen you both work,' he told them.

'It didn't feel like hard work,' said Zac, his eyes shining and his cheeks flushed, even though he was panting.

'I think we're going to have something really special for the show programme,' said Brock, nodding firmly. 'But it's going to take a lot of polish to get it into shape.'

'We can do it,' said Tania. Zac grinned at her.

'Good work, you two,' said Brock. 'Tania, you go and

get changed.' He held something out to Zac. 'Zac, this came in the morning post for you. They just brought it over from the front desk.'

'For me?' Zac was surprised. 'Cool, thanks.'

Tania headed to the locker room, almost oblivious to the waving from Libby across the rink. 'Meet you upstairs!' Libby was yelling, but all Tania could think was, *He's got the letter! Is this going to work?* As she rounded the corner, she saw that Zac was tearing open the envelope . . .

In the locker room, Tania suddenly felt nervous. What if Zac saw through the plan? Her fingers shook as she undid the laces. Would he be pleased? Or would he feel offended? Would he be suspicious?

She was so absorbed in thought that she didn't even hear Zac come in, and jumped a mile when she suddenly saw him standing in the doorway. 'Hi!' Her voice sounded absurdly squeaky. She coughed. 'Uh – everything OK?'

Zac looked stunned, the letter still in his hand. 'Yeah,' he said in a strange voice. 'Tania, you'll never guess what.'

Tania did her best to look concerned. 'Is something wrong?'

'No . . .' Zac blinked and frowned. 'This letter – the one that came for me in the post? It's . . . it's offering me some money for my skating. I mean, it says I could be eligible for a grant.'

'A grant?' Tania tried to look as though she didn't know what he was talking about. 'What sort of grant?'

'It says it's for promising skaters. You can be nominated by anyone – the letter doesn't say who put my name forward. Here, you read it.' He thrust the letter at her.

Tania looked down at it, though she knew the words on the page by heart. After all, she and her mother had spent a whole evening composing it, and then Caroline had gone to print it on some official-looking paper. 'Wow.'

'I know.' Zac still looked stunned. 'You don't think . . . it couldn't be some kind of scam, could it? My parents are always getting things in the post saying they've won a new TV or something.'

'Oh, no, I don't think so,' Tania said quickly. 'After all, it's from a proper organization, isn't it?'

'Is it? I've never heard of the Parchester Ice Association, have you?'

'Oh yes,' blurted Tania. 'I know all about them. I've – er – had a grant myself in the past.'

'Really?' For the first time, a glimmer of hope appeared in Zac's eyes. 'It's a real deal?'

'Yeah, of course.'

'It's a thousand pounds, Tania,' said Zac. He swallowed. 'A thousand pounds! All that money!'

A thousand pounds had never sounded like that much to Tania, but she could see just how much it meant to Zac. 'You could buy new skates,' she said, as though it had only just occurred to her.

He nodded. 'I know. I can't believe it. I honestly thought I would have to give up skating with you. I could never have got together that much money for new skates.' His eyes suddenly narrowed. 'Hang on a minute. Did you have something to do with this?'

'What?' Tania panicked.

Zac didn't look angry though, more amused. 'Was it you who put my name forward for the grant?'

'No,' said Tania. 'Honest. I didn't.' *Which isn't exactly a lie*, she told herself, *because there isn't a grant at all*.

Zac looked at her for a moment, head on one side. It was clear he didn't believe her. Then, with three strides, he was in front of her and his strong arms were round her, hugging her to him. 'Thank you,' he said in her ear. 'Just – thanks.'

Tania's breath had caught in her throat. The sudden

warmth of Zac's body made her dizzy. 'I didn't have anything to do with it,' she protested weakly.

'Yeah, yeah.' Zac let go of her, and grinned. 'Course you didn't. Listen – will you come and help me choose my skates? If I get the money? I haven't got a clue where to start.'

'I'd love to.'

Zac sat down on the bench and started to unlace his boots. 'I'll post the reply tonight. They say I can have the money within a week if I qualify. All I have to do is take the postal orders to the post office and get cash in return. I could be wearing new skates this time next week!'

Tania joined him, sitting on her hands so he couldn't see them trembling. She glanced at Zac's bandaged foot. 'The new ones shouldn't do that to you either, not once they're properly broken in.'

'Oh, I hardly notice this now.' Zac straightened the bandage. 'It's not as bad as it looks. Besides, I never feel injuries while I'm skating. Isn't that the same for everyone?'

Tania opened her mouth to say no, she'd been hurt several times while skating and had felt every twinge, but that wasn't completely true.

'You had a nasty fall today,' said Zac. 'Is your knee OK?'

Tania had forgotten it, but she peeled back her leggings to reveal a large swelling bruise. 'It hurts now,' she said.

'But it didn't before,' said Zac. 'Me too.' He reached out a hand, and gently touched the side of the bruise. 'You should get some ice on that to stop it getting any worse.'

Tania was very aware of how close they were sitting. Zac's arm brushed hers, and she could feel the heat from his leg on her own.

'Tania . . .' said Zac, very quietly. She lifted her face to his. His eyes were large and solemn. She felt as if she were falling into them. His hand brushed a stray strand of hair away from her cheek. Zac's gaze moved down to her lips. 'Um . . .' he said, but his voice shook.

Time stopped. Tania couldn't move – wouldn't have wanted to, even if she could. It was as though she was being pulled irresistibly towards Zac. She leaned closer . . . her eyes began to close . . . his hand stroked her cheek . . .

'Tania!' came Brock's voice. 'Your excitable friend is waiting for you!'

Libby! thought Tania. *Not now!*

Zac's hand fell away. He blinked, and pulled back. 'Uh . . .' he said. 'You'd better . . .'

Tania looked away, blushing furiously. 'Right,' she said. 'See you tomorrow then.'

'Yeah. I'll let you know when I hear about this grant thing.'

'Cool. Fine. Well, er – have a nice evening.'

'You too.'

Chapter 14

don't let go of him

'He nearly kissed you!' Libby was contrite. 'And I blew it for you! I'm so sorry! You must hate me for ever!' The two of them walked out of the building together, Tania glancing around anxiously to make sure no one could hear their conversation. 'Me and my big mouth! I ruined everything, I'm so sorry!'

'Of course you didn't,' Tania told her. 'Maybe it was a good thing you interrupted. Him and me . . . well.'

'What?'

Tania tried to look as though she didn't care. 'It wouldn't really work, would it? We're so different.'

Libby's jaw dropped. 'What's that got to do with anything? He's *gorgeous*! And wow – when he skates – I mean, *wow*! Of course, you're really good too,' she added hastily.

Tania couldn't help but laugh. 'Thanks.'

'I *meant*,' said Libby carefully, 'that I'm used to seeing you be amazing on the ice. But he was doing stuff I've never seen before. And making it look so easy too! I think you're a perfect match.'

'Do you really?'

Libby put an arm around her friend. 'Yes, I do. And now you know he likes you too. Oh, I think I'm going to cry! It's so romantic!'

'Libby, you're being silly . . . '

'And you know what?' Libby suddenly broke away. 'He's good for you. Not just skating, but good for *you*. You're a lot nicer since he's been on the scene.'

'Nicer?' Tania felt hurt. 'What do you mean?'

'Well, you know how I said you never came out with us any more, and how you were getting so serious and, like, *stressed* all the time? It's as if that Tania has gone and a new friendlier one is around.' She looked searchingly at her friend. 'You told me about being scared. Of falling. Are you scared now?'

'Not so much.'

Libby nodded. 'It's Zac, isn't it? I don't know how, but he's helped you through it.'

Tania blushed. 'Yes. He has.'

Libby sighed. 'There you go – a match made in heaven! It's like a fairy tale! Next thing you know, you'll be skating at midnight, all lit up by a mirror ball, and . . .' Her expression suddenly changed. 'Oh good grief, what time is it?'

'Uh . . . just after six?'

'I have to go!' Libby exclaimed, reaching into her bag and scrabbling furiously.

'What's the matter?'

'Have you got a lipstick?'

'What? No, I–'

'I'm supposed to be meeting Scott!' Libby cried. 'I said I'd watch his band rehearsal!'

'Band?'

'Yeah, he's the singer. He looks so hot when he sings, Tan, you wouldn't believe it.' Libby stopped for a moment and considered. 'Though actually, he's not quite as hot as Zac, now I come to think of it . . . ' She caught sight of Tania's expression and laughed. 'Don't worry, I'm not going to steal him from you. Besides, from what just *nearly* happened, I don't suppose I'd stand a chance.' She gave Tania a quick hug. 'See you tomorrow. Sweet dreams.' She giggled and dashed out of the car park.

Tania walked slowly over to where her mum was waiting in the car, head down over the newspaper. The recent conversation with Libby was vanishing out of her memory already – all she could think about was Zac's face, dizzyingly close, and the thought that one more second, just one tiny second, and his lips would have met hers. And Tania wished that Libby hadn't chosen this very day to come and watch the session.

♥

Zac was nervous. 'Do I look normal?' he whispered to Tania, glancing around the street.

'No, you look paranoid. What's the matter?'

'I've got a thousand pounds in cash in my pocket. *In cash*, Tania. For God's sake don't let me get mugged. I still can't believe the money is in *cash*. The woman at the post office looked at me like I'd robbed a bank when I handed over the postal orders. Four for two hundred and fifty each! It took her about half an hour to count all the money out! If I wasn't holding it with my own hand, I wouldn't believe it was real.'

'Calm down. We're going straight into the shop, right? It's not as if we're going to wander around waving it at people.' Tania, grinning, pushed open the door.

'I don't even know where to start,' muttered Zac as he took in the shelves and shelves of boots, blades, guards, cloths, tape . . . 'I've never seen half this stuff before.'

'We start with *him*,' said Tania, pointing at a sales

assistant, who looked up. A smile flashed across his face and he hurried over, giving Tania a hug that lifted her off her feet.

'Tania Dunn, well I never!'

'Hello, Stu,' said Tania. 'Didn't think you'd remember me.'

Stu spread his hands expressively. 'How could anyone forget you?'

'That's not necessarily a compliment.' Tania poked him in the ribs. 'This is Zac.'

'Uh-huh . . . ?' said Stu meaningly.

'He's my skating partner,' said Tania, shooting Stu a look that said, 'Don't even think about saying he's my boyfriend.'

Stu's plucked eyebrows rose into his hairline. 'Your partner? Tania, since when did you go pairs?'

'She hasn't,' Zac said, sticking out his hand for Stu to shake. 'She's been forced to take me under her wing and polish me up. Only for another month though.'

'I *see*,' said Stu. 'Well, aren't you the lucky one? Plenty of boys who'd give their right arms to be in your skates.'

'I know,' said Zac. He glanced at Tania, who tried not to blush. She'd spent most of the previous night wondering what it would be like to kiss him.

'Well,' said Stu, his sharp eyes missing nothing of the exchange, 'what can I do for you today?'

'Zac needs new skates,' said Tania. 'Boots, blades – the lot.'

'Are we talking your skating level?' said Stu, his eyes narrowing. 'Couple of hours a day, advanced jumps, all that?'

'Yes.'

'Right,' said Stu. 'You don't want to be looking at these shelves then.' He put an arm round Zac's shoulders, which was difficult as Stu was a good six inches shorter. 'Come through here . . .'

Tania followed them into the back room, which was twice as big as the front room and crammed from floor to ceiling with boots. Zac's eyes widened further. 'Good grief.'

'What do you usually wear?' asked Stu. 'Reidell? Risport?'

'Umm . . .'

Tania came to the rescue. 'He's been wearing a second-hand pair,' she said firmly. 'This will be his first pair of brand-new boots.'

Stu looked surprised, but Tania's glare prevented him from asking more questions. Instead, he said brightly, 'Right then. Better get you measured up and see what you like.'

Stu became the model of efficiency, measuring Zac's feet to within a millimetre, explaining about the different stiffness of boot, 'See, these are less flexible but give your ankle more support in the double and triple jumps,' and pulling boot after boot off shelves for Zac to try. Soon the floor was littered with items.

'I thought they came with the blades attached,' said Zac.

'No no no.' Stu waved his hands. 'Boots and blades are bought separately at this level.'

'How much do they all cost then?'

Stu shrugged. 'How long is a piece of string? Up to a thousand pounds per pair of boots – blades extra, remember – and over that if you want them custom-made.' He glanced at Tania. 'Yours are all custom-made now, aren't they?'

Tania felt uncomfortable, knowing that her custom boots and blades cost way more than the thousand pounds Zac was about to spend. 'Yes, in America. I send them the measurements and they send me the boots.'

'You should really do the same,' Stu told Zac, 'but if you're doing this show then you won't have time to wait for them.'

Zac was looking bewildered and a little alarmed. 'I can't spend that much.'

'How much have you got?' asked Stu bluntly.

'A thousand pounds,' said Zac, colouring.

'Any flexibility on that?' asked Stu.

'No,' replied Zac firmly. 'That's everything – all in.'

'Ooookay,' said Stu. 'Then we'd better get thinking and sorting. 'Cos you want to leave a bit over for hard and soft guards, maybe a bag, cleaning cloth – all that malarkey.'

'Don't worry,' Tania told Zac. 'Stu's an expert. He'll make it work.'

'Course I will.' Stu winked. 'And I might even invoke my employee privileges and see if I can get you a bit of a discount.'

Zac squirmed. 'I don't want any special treatment.'

Stu looked astonished. '*All* my customers get special treatment,' he told Zac, almost sounding offended. 'But Tania's friends are more special than most.'

'Stu fitted my first pair of skates,' Tania said.

'She was this high,' Stu added, indicating a point on his own leg. 'And didn't say a word.'

'You were very kind,' said Tania.

Stu waved a dismissive hand. 'I get all sorts in here,' he said. 'Shy, loud, naughty. You were a very quiet one. To start with, that is. By the time you were coming for your third pair, I couldn't shut you up!'

'Stu . . .'

'I'm serious!' Stu turned to Zac. 'In all my years of working here, I never saw a child more excited about skating. Couldn't stop talking about it – waltz jump this, mohawk that. Lived and breathed it, didn't you?' He put an arm around Tania. 'I thought then – if any child has the potential to be a star, she has.'

'We're meant to be buying Zac's boots,' Tania reminded him.

'Of course! Yes.' Stu sprang into action.

An hour later, Zac and Tania walked out of the shop, Zac clutching a large canvas bag full of accessories and a slip of paper telling him when his new skates would be ready. 'We'll do a rush job,' Stu told him, 'to fix the blades. Should be able to pick them up in twenty-four hours.'

'Thanks so much,' said Tania, giving Stu a hug.

'Is he good?' he whispered in her ear.

'Very,' she whispered back.

'Then don't let go of him,' Stu told her. 'Anyone can skate on their own; it's so rare to find a good partner.'

'What did he say to you?' asked Zac curiously as they walked away.

Tania felt buoyed up with a wild excitement. She had just spent a thousand pounds on Zac and he had no idea! And it had made him happier than she'd ever seen him. A naughty grin spread over her face. 'He said he fancied you.'

Zac turned white. 'He never!'

'You did guess he was gay, didn't you?'

'Well . . .' said Zac, shifting his new bag from one shoulder to the other. 'I wasn't sure.'

Tania laughed and relented. 'Don't worry,' she said. 'He doesn't fancy you really. He was just saying good luck for the show.'

Zac relaxed. 'Whew! You got me there.'

'You're so easy to wind up,' Tania teased.

Zac laughed. 'He's a bit mad, isn't he?'

'I've known Stu for years,' said Tania. 'He's the best.'

'He seemed to know his stuff,' said Zac. 'Those skates are amazing.' He chewed his lip. 'I don't know what I would have done without that grant. A thousand pounds gone, just like that!'

'I don't think anyone had ever paid in cash before.' Tania giggled. 'Stu looked a bit stunned.'

'But so much money!' said Zac. 'On skates! These had better last me years. I'll never be able to afford another pair.'

Tania looked thoughtful. 'You remember I said you could earn money in competitions, don't you?'

Zac shook his head. 'Yeah, I know, but . . . I've only

been skating for two years. I'm not good enough.' He
glanced at her. 'Am I?'

Tania hesitated. 'I don't know. But you're way better
than you used to be. And your jumps are better than
mine.'

'I don't have the control though. Or the precision.'

'That's just practice. Look how far you've come
already. You could start local. There are county
championships, and then regional and national. You'd
stand a really good chance against the other boys.'

Zac's gaze hit her own. 'I don't think I'd want to
compete solo.'

Tania was going to reply but her breath seemed to
have been sucked away. What was he saying? Did he
want to carry on skating with her? But that wasn't the
deal . . . she was a solo skater.

Wasn't she?

♥

Stu was as good as his word and Zac's new skates
were ready for the next day. 'Wear them in slowly,'
Brock warned him. 'Otherwise you'll bust your
feet. Just a few minutes for the first couple of days.
And wear them at home, around the house. On
carpet.'

'My parents are going to love that,' said Zac, grinning.

'I mean it,' said Brock. 'Don't do anything complicated on the ice until they're properly broken in.'

'How long will it take?'

'Ten days,' Brock said firmly. 'So don't throw out the old skates before then. Right, let's see what we can do with this programme.'

The three of them worked hard on the choreography. 'This is going to be different from anything else in the show,' Brock called over to them at one point.

'Is that a good thing?' Zac whispered to Tania.

'Look at his face,' Tania said. 'His smile couldn't be any bigger. He loves your ideas.'

'But are they any good?' said Zac. 'I mean, skateboarding is all very well on a board . . .'

'They're good,' said Tania, and was surprised to find she meant it. 'Honestly. It's cool to be doing something other than axels and sit spins – I mean, to mix up the usual tricks with something completely fresh.'

'Do you really like the programme?' Zac looked hard at her. 'There's no point doing it if you're not comfortable.'

'I am,' said Tania. 'I didn't think I would be, but I am. I really like this programme – it's the most fun I've had in ages.'

They smiled at each other, and Tania felt her heart thump harder. Looking into his eyes now – she could hardly do it without wanting to lean in closer. But Zac had made no move to kiss her since the time they'd been interrupted, and she couldn't help the dreaded thought that perhaps he hadn't meant to in the first place. *Maybe he's decided it was a mistake?* Something deep inside ached at the thought.

'Tania?' shouted Brock. 'You in another world? Did you hear what I just said?'

Tania blinked, and realized that she'd been standing in a daze for some moments whilst Zac and Brock were deep in discussion at the other end of the rink. She skated over. 'Sorry, what?'

'I said,' Brock repeated patiently, 'that we need a big finish. You got any ideas?'

'Um . . . a pair spin?'

'We've got one of those earlier,' said Zac. 'And we used up the death spiral towards the beginning.' He frowned. 'I don't suppose . . .'

'What?'

Brock tilted his head. 'You got something, Zac?'

'Well . . .' Zac looked apologetically at Tania. 'Tania might not like it.'

'What is it?'

Zac took a deep breath. 'You can't get much bigger than an overhead lift.'

Tania's heart thudded. 'What kind of overhead lift?' she asked, trying to sound calm.

Zac screwed up his eyes. 'A tabletop?' he suggested.

Brock's eyes gleamed. 'That's a very hard lift to pull off, Zac. Very difficult indeed. And dangerous. It would be a fantastic finish to the programme. You think you could do it?'

'Yes,' said Zac. 'But only if Tania wants to.'

Tania felt the familiar panic creeping back. 'You can't lift me over your head,' she said with a half-laugh. 'I'm far too heavy.'

Zac laughed. 'You? You weigh almost nothing, look at you! Besides, all this lifting in practices has made me stronger than I was two months ago.'

Tania bit her lip and looked at Brock. He gazed steadily back. 'It's your call, Tania. It's pretty much as dangerous as you can get. If you fall from that height, it can mean a serious injury.'

A loud crack, a high scream . . . no! Tania shut her eyes. *You've overcome this! Don't go back there!*

Brock's voice was level. 'On the other hand, it's a stunning end to an amazing programme. And underneath you, you'd have one of the best skating partners I've ever coached.'

Zac flushed.

'I'm not kidding,' said Brock, seeing Zac's face. 'You've improved beyond belief in such a short space of time. You're careful with the lifts, you always make sure you land her well, but you're strong and secure now that you've stopped launching yourself into things without thinking.' He turned to Tania. 'And you – you've improved too. Look at the tricks you've been pulling the last week or so. Back in the summer you'd never have dared try them. You'd have tensed up; you'd have botched them. But the fear is leaving you. You're more open to new ideas; you're tackling more complex sequences and leaps. A tabletop lift would be the high point of everything you've achieved recently.' He coughed. 'No pun intended.'

Tania took a deep breath. She knew Brock was right. She knew she was stronger; less scared; more willing to try new things. And it was all down to Zac and his encouragement. But a tabletop lift? She would be supported only by Zac's hands at her waist – held straight over his head, as he travelled round the rink. She'd be – what? Two metres off the ground? That was a long way to fall. She looked at Zac, and although he was avoiding her eyes, she suddenly knew she would do it. *I'd trust him with my life*, she thought, and a wave of warmth crashed over her. She nodded.

'You sure, Tania?' said Brock, watching her carefully.

'Yes. I'm sure. I want to try it.' She smiled. 'Besides, you're right. It would be the best moment in the programme. People would talk about it afterwards.' *Like they used to talk about my programmes, back when I was on top of my game. Before they started to whisper and gossip that I'd lost my edge. This would show them!*

Brock looked pleased. 'Good. If you feel uncomfortable, we can take it out.'

Zac reached for Tania's hand. 'I won't let you down,' he said.

There was a pause, and Brock's mouth twitched. Tania gave a small snort, and the next second they were all laughing fit to burst. 'I didn't mean that,' spluttered Zac. 'I meant I wouldn't get it wrong – oh, never mind . . .'

♥

'It's a bit scary,' admitted Tania to Libby. 'It's a really long way up. But Zac is very strong. I just have to stay focused.'

Libby was scrabbling around in her bag. 'Where's my phone? I must get some tickets. I wish you'd been trying this lift thing when I was watching, it sounds brilliant!'

Tania couldn't help smiling. 'Everything's good at the moment.'

I must have left it at home,' Libby went on, practically stuffing her head inside her bag. She sighed. 'Never mind. Has he kissed you yet then?'

'Libby . . .'

'What?' Libby gave her a grin. 'Come on, you can tell me.'

'There hasn't been time,' Tania said, fiddling with her hair. 'We're never alone. Brock's always there, or other skaters.'

'You should tell him how you feel about him.'

'But what if he doesn't feel the same way?' Tania's expression was appalled. 'I mean, maybe he just thinks of me as a friend, or his skating partner?' She stopped as a thought struck her.

'What is it?' asked Libby, seeing her hesitate.

'It's probably nothing . . . only he did say he didn't want to skate solo. In competitions, I mean.' Tania glanced up at her friend. 'Do you think that means he wants to carry on skating with *me*?'

Libby pulled a comical face. 'How would I know? You're never going to find out unless you ask him, Tania.'

'It's too close to the show,' Tania said, shaking her head. 'I can't do it. It might mess everything up.'

'But hang on a minute.' Libby held up a hand. 'I thought *you* were a solo skater. If Zac wants to carry on skating with you – well, that's impossible anyway, isn't it? You've always told me you do singles.'

'I don't know any more,' Tania confessed in a low voice. 'Something in me really doesn't want to go back to skating on my own. But it's so risky, Libby. He's not got my training. What if it all went wrong? Besides, I hardly know anything about him. We only ever talk about skating. What if we're – you know – incompatible or something?'

'Or what if he's already got a girlfriend?'

Tania's eyes opened very wide. 'I hadn't even *thought* of that! Do you think he might?'

'Hmm.' Libby sat down on a step. 'He's at college, right?'

'Yeah, and he's really bright. Physics, psychology and – something else. Hard stuff, I mean. He wants to go to university.'

'And his parents run a pub.'

'Yes.'

'Which pub? Where?'

Tania shrugged helplessly. 'I don't know – I didn't ask.'

Libby gave a sigh of frustration. 'You are a nightmare, Tania Dunn. If it were me, I'd want to find out everything I could about him.'

'I didn't want him to think I was nosy.'

Libby raised her eyebrows. 'Do you *want* to know more about him? I could do it for you, if you like. Find out stuff – I'm good at it.'

'Don't you dare!' Tania was shocked. 'Lib, please, don't get involved. I'm sure things will work out one way or the other.'

Libby looked disappointed. 'I'm very discreet,' she said. 'Honestly, he'd never know.'

'No!'

'Oh, all right. But don't complain you know nothing about him then.'

'I wasn't complaining!'

Libby stuck out her tongue. 'Look who's touchy about her boyfriend now,' she remarked.

'He's not my boyfriend.'

'No, and he never will be if you don't tell him how you feel.' Libby paused, and then said unexpectedly, 'What are you going to wear for the show?'

'Don't know yet.' Tania pulled on her ponytail again. 'Mum and I are going shopping tomorrow. She'll customize whatever we get.'

'How long is it till the show?'

'Two weeks,' said Tania.

Libby looked at her friend. 'Two weeks left with Zac,' she commented. 'And then what?'

Chapter 15

if you want to be the best

'What about that one?' Caroline pointed. 'Halterneck is a great style for you.'

Tania looked at the dress hanging high on the wall. She frowned. 'It's not quite right.'

Her mother sighed. 'We've looked at them all, Tania. Skating dresses don't grow on trees, you know. This is the only shop within sixty miles – unless we order online, and you never like doing that.'

'I like to try them on first,' said Tania.

'Well, we could always order several designs and then send back the ones we don't like.'

'Let's just have another look at this shelf,' said Tania.

'Remember,' said Caroline, for what felt like the twentieth time, 'it's the shape of the dress we're looking at. I can dye it a different colour, sew stuff onto it – anything you like. You've got to look beyond the way it appears right now.'

'I know,' said Tania. 'I just – this programme is different from anything I've done before. It feels like I should *wear* something different too.'

'Longer skirt?' suggested Caroline. 'One with drapes like flames?'

Tania shook her head. 'Can't have anything too long,' she said. 'I do things like cartwheels. Can't risk it falling over my head or getting caught in a blade.'

'Then are you sure you need a skirt at all?' said Caroline. Tania swung round to stare at her. Caroline shrugged. 'I'm serious. Do you have to have a skirt?'

'What would I have instead?'

'Catsuit,' said Caroline promptly. 'An all-in-one. With stirrups.'

Tania didn't know what to say. 'I've always had a skirt.'

'But you just said this programme is different from everything you've done in the past,' Caroline pointed out. 'And you want to wear something different. So, why not wear a catsuit?'

'It would show *everything*,' Tania muttered.

Caroline laughed. 'Do you really think a little chiffon skirt covers you up? Tania, you know as well as I do how those bits of fabric blow around when you're skating. A fast back crossover, and that skirt rides up so much you may as well not be wearing one at all!'

Tania bit her lip. A catsuit . . . Tania had never worn a catsuit on the ice before. But then, this wasn't the same as her old skating life, was it? This was something new – something daring, dangerous. And if Zac were going to lift her above his head, he'd probably be glad there wasn't a skirt to flop into his eyes . . .

'All right,' said Tania, lifting her gaze to her mother's. 'Let's go for it.'

'Wow.' Caroline laughed. 'I didn't think you'd agree. But you will look amazing, Tania. You've got such a good figure. Everyone will be glued to you.'

Wonder what Zac will think, Tania suddenly thought, and blushed scarlet.

'You all right, sweetie?' Caroline peered at her. 'You've gone all red. Are you hot?'

'Yeah,' said Tania, grateful for the excuse. 'It is a bit stuffy in here.'

'Well, there's no point being in here if we're not buying a skating dress,' said Caroline. She made an apologetic face at the sales assistant. 'Sorry, we've decided to go for something completely different.'

The sales assistant shrugged. 'No problem,' she said in a bored voice.

'She must be new,' Caroline said in a low voice as

they left the shop. 'The last time we were in, there was a lovely girl who was so helpful.'

'Where are you going to get a catsuit?' asked Tania.

'Oh, that's easy,' said Caroline, digging in her bag for her car keys. 'I'll just order one from the dance catalogue. They do next-day delivery. I'll show you the choice – and what colour do you want?'

Tania thought. 'Not white,' she said. 'It makes you look fat. And not black. It's dull.'

'Red?'

'But Zac's got to match, hasn't he?' said Tania. 'I don't think he's keen on red.'

'You've got to stand out,' said Caroline. She brandished her keys triumphantly. 'Here we are! Let's get going.'

Tania got into the car and stared out of the window. Blue? Green? Yellow?

'What colours does Zac like?' asked Caroline. 'What does he usually wear?'

'Grey,' said Tania. 'And navy and black. Like we all do in practice.'

Caroline carefully reversed out of her parking space. 'I meant in shows and competitions. What does he wear then?'

'He's never competed,' said Tania. 'Or been in a show.'

Caroline was surprised. 'I didn't realize. I mean, I knew he hadn't been skating that long, but I thought he'd be working his way through the tests and competitions like you did.' She frowned. 'It doesn't sound as if he's good enough to partner you, if he's not that serious about it.'

'Oh, he's good enough,' said Tania. She gave a sigh. 'He's very good, actually.'

Caroline smiled. 'You said that in a funny voice.' She glanced sideways at her daughter. 'Are you perhaps liking this Zac boy more than you expected?'

'Muuum.'

'I get it,' said Caroline. 'I see now. So *that's* why you've been so keen to go to practice lately!' She grinned. 'Well, well.'

'Don't laugh at me.'

'I'm not.' Caroline reached out to pat Tania's leg. 'I think it's nice that you've found someone who loves skating like you do. And he's certainly having a good effect on you – you've been much easier to get along with recently. And when you said you wanted to buy him skates, I was really impressed. It shows you've started to mature a bit. Be less self-obsessed.'

Tania flushed. 'I'm not self-obsessed,' she mumbled.

Her mother smiled. 'It's all right. That's how it is for

young people, and even more so for you since you've had to concentrate so hard on your skating. You have to be focused if you want to get where you want to be.' She hesitated. 'How does – Zac – feel about you?'

Tania picked at a dirt mark on the window. 'Don't know.'

'Ah, I see.' Caroline negotiated a tricky roundabout and then glanced at her daughter. 'I guess the best time to ask him is after the show, when you're no longer skating together. That way it wouldn't be awkward if he said no.'

'Ye-es.'

Her mother noticed the hesitation in her voice. 'Is there something else?'

'N-not exactly.' Tania took a breath. 'Do you think people can work together and go out at the same time?'

'You mean . . . mix business and personal?' Caroline pulled a face. 'Not very easily, no. But it wouldn't be like that for you, would it? I mean, you're a singles skater. So you wouldn't be working with Zac again anyway.' She reversed into their driveway. 'You're thinking of asking him out before the show, aren't you? It would be better to wait till it's all over. That way you won't have to worry about things going wrong between you.'

Tania reached for the handle, her heart heavy. *Wait till it's all over*, her mother had said. *But what if I don't want it to be over?* she wondered miserably. *What if I want to carry on skating with him and go out with him too? Am I crazy even to think about it?*

♥

'You're not concentrating,' Brock told her. 'You must stay focused.'

Tania nodded.

'Take a break,' Brock said, and disappeared into his office.

Tania stepped off the rink and dropped onto a bench.

'What's going on?' asked Zac, leaning over the barrier. 'You seem a bit spaced out.'

Tania scuffed the floor with her blade. 'Just stuff,' she said lamely. There was no way she could tell him how much she dreaded the show because it meant the end of their skating partnership. She cast around for a possible excuse. 'My mum said something that annoyed me.'

'Oh, right.' Zac seemed at a loss. 'Are you OK?'

Tania shrugged. 'It's nothing really. Doesn't your mum get on your back sometimes too?'

'Not really. She's too busy working.' Zac laughed. 'They don't even know I'm in the show.'

Tania looked up, startled. 'Haven't you told them?'

'Sort of,' said Zac. 'I mean, I've mentioned it once or twice. But they're busy. If they're not actually serving customers, they're cleaning up, or ordering new supplies, or filling in health and safety forms. And then they have to sleep a bit.'

'You work there sometimes, right?' Tania wondered if this was a good time to try to find out more about him. *Ask him questions!* she could hear Libby order her.

'Yeah.' Zac swivelled on his new skates. 'When I'm not here or at college. I have to – they need reliable staff. You wouldn't believe the number of people who just don't turn up for their shifts. It's mad. You'd think people would be glad of the pay, but they think working in a pub is a rubbish job, so they don't bother to treat it with respect. And then they complain when they get fired!' He shook his head. 'I tell you, running a pub is way harder than skating. Sometimes I feel guilty about having so much fun here.'

Tania's forehead crinkled. 'I'd never thought of it like that,' she said slowly. 'I mean, skating has always been something I love doing, but it's hard work too. I wouldn't have called it fun exactly. Long hours, and

you get so tired, and you never get to see friends . . .'
She tailed off.

'Sounds like the pub,' Zac said at the same time as
Tania said, 'I guess it's like your parents.'

They grinned at each other. 'But we don't have
abusive customers,' Zac pointed out.

'Just an abusive coach,' said Tania.

Zac laughed. 'True.'

'Uh-oh,' said Zac, spotting Brock heading over.
'Looks like that's our break over.'

'I've been thinking,' Brock said without preamble.
'The ending's all wrong.'

Zac looked puzzled. 'But that's our big lift.'

'No, not that.' Brock waved an arm. 'The fish dive
out of the lift. I don't like it. It's too showy.'

Tania and Zac exchanged glances. 'But it's for a
show,' Tania said hesitantly. 'I mean . . .'

'I know what you mean. But it's not right for this
programme,' said Brock. 'It's too outward. I want to
try something different.'

'We can't get out of the lift any other way,' said Zac.
'We've tried.'

'No, you can keep the fish dive,' said Brock, 'but I
want you to look at each other, not at the audience.'

Tania was puzzled. 'I'm at the wrong angle.'

'No, no,' said Brock. 'Let me explain it.'

They practised for fifteen minutes before Brock was satisfied. 'That's better,' he said.

Tania felt a slight quiver of nervousness. Brock's new position for them had Tania looking up over her outstretched arm to Zac, who was bent towards her. Her hand was brushing his cheek, and the whole position felt incredibly intimate. 'Look into his eyes,' Brock had told her. 'No, you're looking past his ear. The audience needs to see the connection.'

But I'm not supposed to have a connection, Tania thought in a panic. *Not until after the show, according to Mum. In case it ruins everything. And if I look at Zac, everyone will know. When I look into his eyes, I can't help myself. Everyone will be able to see how I feel about him! Even HE must be able to see!*

'It's a bit weird,' said Zac. 'I mean, for an ending. Are you sure it works?'

Tania held her breath.

Brock nodded. 'Absolutely. It's so much stronger than the previous ending. I wish you could see it from the front. You two have chemistry. It's a great skating partnership.'

Tania's cheeks flamed, and she tried not to glance at Zac. There was an awkward pause – or was it just awkward because Tania felt so embarrassed?

Zac cleared his throat. 'The song helps.'

He's trying to say we don't really have chemistry, thought Tania in a panic. *He's saying it's all about the music. He doesn't feel that way about me after all!*

'In what way?' asked Brock.

'Well, the lyrics could almost be about us – about Tania anyway.'

'About me?'

'Yeah.' Zac turned to her and she desperately hoped she wasn't too red in the face. 'All that stuff about coming out the other side after a battle. It always makes me think of you on that rope net, freezing up. And then how you came down that zip-wire as though you were just floating through the air.' He grinned. 'When the river was deep, you didn't falter.'

'That's because she had you to catch her,' said Brock unexpectedly. 'He's right, you know Tania, I hadn't realized how closely the lyrics fitted you.' He laughed. 'Though you weren't exactly drawn together through destiny – I think I had more than a little to do with that!'

Chapter 16

it's only money

'So your mum said it would be OK to date Zac?' asked Libby.

'Basically, yes. As long as we weren't skating together.'

'But you won't be after the show anyway, will you?' Libby nodded happily. 'So that works out just fine.' Then she saw the look on Tania's face. 'Oh no. Oh, hang on a minute. This isn't what I think it is, is it?'

'What do you mean?'

'You want to keep on skating with him, don't you?' Libby peered at her. 'That's it. You want to skate pairs with him. *And* go out with him.'

'I don't know!'

'Yes, you do. I can see it all over your face. Oh, Tania.' Libby looked sympathetic. 'Didn't I say you'd understand when it happened to you? The thunderbolt, I mean. It takes over, doesn't it?'

Tania sagged. 'I don't know what to do.'

'But why are you worrying? From what you said the other day, Zac wants to keep on skating with you too. So isn't this a good thing?'

'Not if Mum won't let me . . .'

'Oh, for goodness' sake!' exclaimed Libby. 'Since when have you ever let anyone get in your way before? Come on, Tania, this is *you* we're talking about. If you want something, you have to go for it. And if I know you, you'll get it too. Your mum will come round.' She sighed. 'At least Zac's straightforward. I mean, you get the feeling he wouldn't mess you around. Not like *some* boys I could mention.'

'How's it going with Scott?' asked Tania, glad of the opportunity to change the subject.

Libby made a frustrated noise. 'I don't know. I never know where I am with him. Like yesterday, for example. He said he wanted to spend time with me, but when I said, how about this evening?, he said no, he had a band practice.'

'Didn't he?'

'Well, I believed him,' said Libby, 'but then I saw Tom – the drummer – out in town. Right around the time Scott had told me the band was practising.'

'Perhaps Tom had something important to do in

town and couldn't make the rehearsal,' suggested Tania.

Libby sighed. 'Yeah, you're probably right. I just feel something's wrong. But maybe I'm imagining things.'

Tania put an arm around her friend. 'I'm sure everything's fine. Scott would be mad to mess you around.'

'Aw, Tania, you're so sweet.' Libby leaned in to her shoulder and sighed again. 'I wish you could come out sometime. We used to go to the cinema, didn't we?'

'Let's go again,' said Tania, surprising herself. 'After the show's over.'

Libby stared. 'Are you serious?'

'Why not? I won't have to put in so many hours at the rink, not until my next test, anyway. It would be fun.'

Libby broke into a beaming smile. 'You sure? That would be awesome! I can't wait! Oooh! Speaking of which, I got my tickets yesterday.'

'Tickets for what?'

'Tickets for your show, silly. On Saturday. Less than a week to go!' Libby nudged Tania in the ribs. 'Can't wait to see this amazingly romantic routine. I'm taking Scott. He won't know what's hit him.'

Her face fell. 'Assuming he hasn't dumped me by then, that is.'

♥

'What do you think?'

Zac made a face. 'It's a bit sparkly, isn't it?'

Tania rolled her eyes. 'Costumes are supposed to be sparkly, Zac.'

'Well, yeah.' Zac fingered the shirt, with its diagonal swirls of electric blue sequins. 'I thought yours would be sparkly. Not mine.'

'But we have to match,' said Tania. 'You'll be fine.'

'I'll feel stupid,' Zac grumbled. 'Can't I wear it without the sequins?'

Tania was amused. 'No, you can't. My mum stayed up all night sewing those on. And if you complain, she'll add even more.'

'No!' Zac held up his hands. 'Not more sequins!'

Tania laughed. 'She's had to do everything in a rush because my catsuit was late in the post.'

'Your what?'

'Catsuit.' Tania held it out. 'It's an all-in-one.'

Zac's eyes widened. 'You can fit into that?' he said. 'It looks like an outfit for a six-year-old.'

'It's stretchy,' Tania told him.

Zac fingered the silky material. 'Doesn't look like it's going to cover you up much.' His face suddenly flamed bright red.

Tania knew her own face was blushing in response. 'Oh well,' she said stupidly, 'at least you'll know where to put your hands.' *Oh God!* she thought to herself. *I can't believe I just said that!*

Zac coughed loudly and bent to lace his boots. Tania noticed his fingers shook slightly, and it made her stomach feel all squirmy. 'Well,' he said, and cleared his throat. 'I guess you have to wear sparkly stuff and – and so on. But I don't see why I have to too. People will laugh at me.'

Tania shook her head. 'Not when they see you skate.'

Zac made a disbelieving noise.

'I'm serious,' said Tania. 'As soon as you start moving, they won't notice your costume any more. Especially when they see some of your moves. Trust me.'

Zac looked embarrassed but pleased. 'I suppose it still feels weird to hear you compliment me. You've been skating for so much longer. I sort of – admire you.'

'Well.' Tania didn't know where to look. The room felt hotter with every passing minute. 'You shouldn't.

In some ways you're just as good as me, maybe even better.' There was a pause, and Tania felt she would burst if something didn't happen. She stood up. 'You coming?'

It was an excellent practice. Even Brock could find little to criticize in the programme. 'That overhead lift is cracking,' he said. 'Really cracking. It's going to bring the house down.'

'As long as it doesn't bring *me* down,' joked Tania.

'No chance,' said Brock. 'You're solid as a rock up there.' He shifted his bag onto his shoulder. 'Right, so you've got your costumes and all that sorted?'

Tania giggled. 'Zac doesn't like his sequins.'

'Tough,' said Brock. 'I want you guys here every evening as usual this week, even though I may not always have time to run your programme. There's too much stuff going on for the show.'

'No problem,' said Zac.

'Right,' said Brock. 'I'll see you both tomorrow, though I can't say what time.'

Tania and Zac headed towards the gap in the rink barrier. 'Oh, Brock,' said Zac, as though the thought had only just occurred to him, 'do you think the Parchester Ice Association would sponsor me if I decided to compete?' Tania froze.

'The who?' asked Brock, his attention elsewhere.

'The Parchester Ice Association.'

Brock shook his head. 'Never heard of them. You must have got your names mixed up.'

The bell rang to signify the end of one session and the beginning of the next. A group of eager primary-school-age children leaped onto the ice, pushing past Zac, who was standing stock-still, a puzzled expression on his face.

'Come on,' Tania called, her insides churning with fear. 'We've got to get off the ice.' Suddenly she was babbling. 'There's this new muffin they've got in the café, it's raspberry and white chocolate, do you want to grab one on the way out? Because it looks really nice . . .'

Zac stepped off the ice, his hand gripping the barrier just that little bit too hard. 'Wait. Wait a minute.'

'But they only had a couple left when I checked earlier, so we should really—'

'*Stop!*'

Tania's words shuddered to a halt. The air whispered in her lungs. *Not now, oh please, not now . . .*

Zac was standing staring at the floor, his face strangely pale. 'That letter . . .' he said. 'It was a scam, after all . . . but it couldn't have been because the money really arrived . . .' He shook his head. 'No, it was real. But the Parchester Ice Association doesn't exist . . .'

'Brock must have misheard you,' suggested Tania.

'No, he didn't.' Zac stared hard at her. 'You said they were a real organization. You said you'd had a grant from them before.'

'Well, maybe it wasn't from them. I can't remember.'

'*You can't remember?*' Zac repeated in a hard tone. 'What do you mean?'

Tania hugged herself. 'Look, Zac, does it really matter?' She tried to laugh but the sound cracked in the icy air. 'I mean, you got the money, didn't you? Does it really matter where it came from?'

'Of course it matters!' snapped Zac. 'I'm not taking money off someone without knowing why or who. I should give it back.'

'M-maybe they don't want it back,' stammered Tania. 'The person who gave it to you, I mean. Maybe they want you to have it . . .' She trailed off.

As soon as his eyes met hers, she knew it was all over. 'It was *you*, wasn't it?' he said bluntly.

Tania looked around desperately but there was no escape. And there were at least six parents within earshot who were giving her curious looks. 'Can we talk about this somewhere–'

'*Who paid for my skates, Tania?*'

'I – I did.'

'You paid a thousand pounds for my skates.'

'Yes.'

He stared at her for a long moment. Tania cringed before the blankness in his eyes. 'I – I only meant . . .' she said helplessly. 'I just wanted you to have what I had . . .'

'You felt *sorry* for me,' Zac said.

'Yes – no! It wasn't like that.'

'What was it like, then?'

Tania took a shaky breath. 'I've always had everything,' she said. 'You – you're a really good skater. You needed skates. I wanted to carry on skating with you.'

'So this was a career move,' said Zac.

'No! No, of course not! It just seemed crazy that I had the money for the skates but you'd have to stop because you didn't. It wasn't fair.'

'So you thought you'd make it right,' said Zac, but his voice was hard. 'By helping out the charity case.'

'No, I . . .'

'You know what's most humiliating?' he went on, oblivious to the interested glances they were attracting. 'You know what's the worst thing? I thought we were becoming – friends. Well, maybe more than friends.

I thought I had proved myself on the ice to you; that you considered me an equal. And now I find that all the time, you carried on thinking of me as inferior.'

'That's not true!'

'So why didn't you offer me the money direct?' asked Zac, his voice ringing across the rink. 'Why this stupid lie about a made-up organization?'

'Because I knew you were too proud to take the money!' cried Tania.

There was a sudden silence, and they both realized everyone on the ice had turned to look. Brock was heading over, his expression unreadable. 'I don't know what all this is about,' he said in a low voice that could have cut glass, 'but you two are making a spectacle of yourselves. Get to the lockers, get changed, and get this sorted *outside*.'

Zac's mouth tightened and he strode past Tania. Tania's face was red with humiliation, and she turned to follow him, away from Brock's accusing glare.

Once on the benches, Zac bent to unlace his boots, his fingers trembling with rage so much that he could hardly undo the knots. Tania's knees felt weak: how could she have believed he wouldn't find out? She wanted to say she was sorry, but the words wouldn't come, and in her own way, she felt angry too. Why couldn't he just keep the skates?

'It's only money,' she muttered as Zac finally tugged the boots from his feet and pulled on his trainers.

He looked up at her, and she almost burst into tears at the look in his eyes. 'Only a Chelsea skater would say that,' he said with venom. Then he walked out of the rink, leaving his skates on the wet floor in front of her.

Chapter 17

no wonder he's mad at you

Brock was unsympathetic. 'I can't believe you were so stupid, Tania. If I'd known, I'd have put a stop to it.'

Tania could hardly breathe, she was crying so much. 'I just – wanted – to help,' she hiccupped.

'Well, you've managed to make a complete mess of things,' Brock told her, exasperated. 'And now it looks like I've lost the highlight of the show programme too.'

Tania stared in horror. 'You think Zac won't skate with me?'

Brock threw up his hands. 'He left his boots behind, didn't he? I don't think he's going to forgive you any time soon. You kids! Why do you have to make everything so complicated?'

Tania let out another choking sob. 'I'm so sorry, Brock. I've ruined – everything. And I – never meant to. Can't you – talk to him?'

'And say what?' Brock looked at her, and his tone softened. 'Zac's not some child you can fool. He's a young man. It's no surprise that he reacted like this. He feels you humiliated him.'

'I don't understand!'

Brock sighed. 'Of course you don't. It's because you've never had to worry about that kind of thing. Zac doesn't come from money. His parents have struggled to pay for his skating. He works hard – harder than you ever have.'

Tania felt sulky. 'I work hard.'

'Only at skating,' Brock said. 'Zac works at everything – college, his job – everything. His careers teacher thinks he's good enough to get into a top university.'

'How do you know that?'

Brock shrugged. 'Because I asked him. Tania, I'm very fond of you, always have been. But you live in your own little world. It's important to be focused, but not to the extent that you block out everyone else. Other people have lives too.'

Tania's lip trembled. 'What can I do?'

'Nothing to do with me,' Brock said. 'I told you. You have to figure this one out yourself.' He frowned. 'But do it fast, Tania. The show's on Saturday. I can't afford to lose my top two skaters.'

♥

'Why won't you tell us what's going on?' Caroline looked anxiously at her daughter over the dinner table.

Her husband Alistair frowned. 'Has something happened at the rink?'

Tania shook her head miserably. 'It's nothing. I mean, yes – something did happen, but it's something I've got to sort out.' She poked at her dinner.

Caroline and Alistair exchanged glances. 'It's not something to do with Zac, is it?' said Caroline carefully.

'No,' lied Tania.

'Because you remember what I said about waiting until after the show . . .'

Tania shot a look at her mother. 'Don't worry, Mum. There's absolutely no danger of me and Zac getting together – not now.' Her heart gave an uncomfortable lurch. *And that's true. He'll never trust me again.*

'What happened?' asked Caroline.

Tania put down her knife and fork. 'I'm finished, can I go upstairs?'

'You've hardly touched it,' said Alistair.

Tania shrugged. 'Not very hungry.'

Caroline sighed. 'Oh, all right. If there's nothing we can do to help . . .'

'No,' said Tania. 'Thanks. There isn't.'

Once in her room, Tania threw herself on the bed and stared at the ceiling. When she thought about the events of this afternoon, her eyes filled with tears again. How could things go so horribly wrong so quickly? And how on earth could she ever make them right again?

Libby, Tania thought. *Libby knows about boys. She'll know what to do*.

Libby took a long time to answer her mobile. 'Tania, hi. Sorry, I was just – well, never mind.'

Tania wiped her eyes. 'Is now a good time?'

'Yeah.' Libby sounded a bit distracted. 'Yeah, it's fine. I'm sort of looking out for someone, but it's OK for the moment. Are you all right? You sound funny.'

'No, I'm not OK.' Tania swallowed. 'Zac and I had a kind of argument.'

'Oh no,' said Libby. 'What about?'

'Well, it's complicated,' said Tania, trying to think how best to explain. 'I did something for him, without him knowing. Something nice, that is. Anyway, he found out, and he got really angry.'

'Why would he be angry if it was something nice?' Libby was puzzled. 'That's a bit weird. What did you do exactly?'

Tania hesitated.

'You still there?' came Libby's voice.

'Yeah,' said Tania. 'Yeah, I – well, I gave him something. But he didn't know it was from me.'

Libby laughed. 'You're going to have to tell me, Tania. What did you give him?'

Tania screwed up her eyes. 'A thousand pounds.'

'A *what*?'

'A thousand pounds.'

There was silence on the line for a moment. Then Libby let out a long breath. 'Whew. Wow, Tania, that's – that's a lot of money. What was it for?'

'New skates.'

'I get it. Wow.' She let out another laugh. 'You've never given *me* a thousand pounds.'

'Libby . . .'

'I'm kidding! But Tania, you can't just go around giving people money like that.'

'Why not?' Tania felt tearful again. 'It's just money, Lib. I've got it, he needs it – why shouldn't I give it to him? What's so wrong with that?'

'Oh, Tania.' Libby sounded sympathetic. 'I know what you're saying, but it doesn't work like that. So what – you pretended it was from some random generous person, did you?'

'Something like that.'

'And now he's found out it was from you.'

'Yes. And he's really mad.'

'Sorry, Tania,' Libby said finally. 'I don't know what to suggest.'

'But I thought you'd have some advice! You know about boys,' pleaded Tania.

'Yeah, I know they like football and toilet jokes,' said Libby sarcastically. 'But this is way out of my league, Tan. And it's not really about Zac anyway, is it? It's sort of about you. Because you don't get why he's mad.'

'That's exactly it! I thought he'd be pleased! And he was, when he heard he'd been given the money. He was so excited about buying the boots and everything. Why does it matter where the money came from?'

Libby sighed. 'All right. Let me think.' She paused for a moment. 'Right. Imagine you're entered for the British championship best skater of the year whatsit.'

Tania snorted.

'Yeah, I know, it's not really called that. Whatever. Say you've got to skate your heart out. You're up against some tough competition. There are three skaters up at the top with you. You've been practising for months and months. You're the best you've ever been. You've got a real chance of winning. With me so far?'

'Yeah, but . . .'

'Then,' said Libby, 'the day before the competition, those three other top skaters – they all get food poisoning.'

'That's so unlikely!'

'No, you're missing the point. Those three skaters can't compete, they're too ill. You go out there, do your stuff, and you win! But you win by a mile. It's too easy. They hand you the trophy, or medal or whatever. You're champion of Britain. But you know what people are saying.'

Tania considered. 'They're saying I only won because the other three didn't turn up.'

'Right.'

'But that's not fair, because I might have won anyway.'

'Right. So what they're saying shouldn't bother you. But it does, because you didn't have to beat the best.'

'Lib, I'm a bit lost,' said Tania.

'The point is,' said Libby, 'Zac works hard for his money. When he gets paid, it means something to him. He has to save up for things he really wants. But when he finally gets them, they mean a lot. If you beat the best, you can feel really proud of what you achieved. But if you win because someone hands it to you on a plate, then isn't it a bit like cheating?'

'Zac called me a Chelsea skater.'

'Well,' said Libby, 'that's a bit unfair. You've worked really hard to get this far in skating. No one can say you've not put in the training. But you haven't ever had to worry about anything else, like money. Not like some people.'

Tania gulped. 'Lib, am I shallow? I mean, do you think I'm vain and self-obsessed and all that? Because I have money?'

'Oh, Tania, do you really think we'd be friends if I thought that?' Libby's voice softened. 'You are kind and sweet and hard-working. It's not your fault that skating takes up so much of your life there's not much left for other things. You live in a kind of bubble. But you're a *good* person, Tan.'

Tania drew a shaky breath. 'Thanks, Lib. You're such a good friend.'

'Yeah, yeah, tell me about it.' Libby sounded as though she was smiling. 'And *you* keep my feet on the ground. You stop me being too crazy and off-the-wall.'

Tania smiled in response. 'That's right. We balance each other out.'

'Exactly,' came Libby's voice. 'Which is why *you're* safe and sound at home, like a sensible girl, and *I'm* hiding behind a blue Volkswagen Golf in the middle of the High Street.'

Tania sat up on her bed. 'You're *where*? Doing *what*? Why are you hiding?'

'I'm following Scott. He went into the music shop fifteen minutes ago, and he's still in there!'

'Why are you following him?'

'Because I think he's cheating on me!' Libby wailed. 'With the girl from the music shop!'

'Are you sure?'

'Of course I'm not sure! That's why I'm following him!' Libby's voice suddenly changed tone. 'Gotta go. He's just come out.'

'Has he bought something?'

'Call you later, Tania.' The phone went dead.

Tania stared at the phone for a moment. Should she call Libby back? But what if she was in the middle of following Scott, and the phone ringing ruined everything? She'd have to wait for Libby to call again.

She lay back on her bed and thought. Libby's story about the skating championships was a bit muddled but Tania thought she could see the point. If she had worked really hard for something, and then someone had come along and told her she didn't need to, she'd won it anyway . . . well, she'd feel a bit cheated, wouldn't she? All that wasted effort. But surely this was different? It wasn't as though Zac would ever have got the money together on his own. Or would he? Had she ever actually asked him if he was saving up?

No wonder, said the voice in Tania's head. *No wonder he's mad at you. You didn't even think about how he might feel. You just wanted to give him the money because it would make you feel good. And it would mean you could carry on skating with him . . .*

It was a restless night.

♥

The next day, Tania went to the rink with her heart thudding in her ears. Would he be there? Her fingers shook so much she could hardly tie her laces, and she had to keep swallowing because her mouth was so dry.

Brock was supervising a group rehearsal. Four young couples were performing a routine to 'Footloose' and Brock was watching with a sharp eye and yelling, 'More swing in those steps! Keep that leg straight, Sian! And for God's sake, look like you're enjoying it!'

He caught her eye as she approached the rink, and shook his head. Tania's heart sank. *He's not here. He's not coming.*

'Is there any point me practising?' Tania said to Brock when she reached him.

Brock's eyes followed one of the couples that had got slightly out of sync with the rest. 'Course there is,' he said shortly. 'There's always a point to practice. He might turn up.' He broke off to shout, 'David, if you can't hear the rhythm, you need to watch the others more!'

'What if he doesn't?' Tania said in a small voice. 'Turn up.'

'Then you will have had a good workout anyway. Now go do something. I'm busy.'

Zac didn't turn up the next day either. Or the day after that. Tania practised some basic figures on her own, but her heart wasn't in it. Every time the main doors banged, Tania's heart thudded and she automatically looked up. Every time it wasn't Zac, she felt slightly sick.

'Can't you find out where he lives and go round on bended knee?' Libby asked one evening. 'Beg him to come back?'

'I don't think it would work,' said Tania sadly. 'You didn't see the look on his face. He hates me.'

Libby gave her friend a hug but she didn't offer any more advice.

Practising on her own reminded Tania how lonely it was. She missed Zac's easy smile, the way he teased her and she was never sure if he was serious or not.

She missed the warmth of his hand in hers and the challenge of matching strokes around the rink. She even missed the lifts.

Each hour dragged, but even though her mind wasn't on the skating, Tania did notice that her technique was stronger than ever. She tried a double axel just to see what happened, and landed it easily. Tania was astonished. She did it again, just to make sure. Whatever had happened in-between, for whatever reason, she was now landing the jumps better than she had for a year. Somehow the fear of falling had gone. *Because of Zac*, she thought. *He's the one who's given me back the courage to try, even if it means risking a fall.* The memory of Kerri's fall was as vivid as ever but somehow she no longer found it crippling. Just because it had happened to Kerri didn't mean it would happen to her. Maybe, just maybe, she'd get up the courage to try a triple axel before too long.

Brock had been right after all. Pairing Tania with Zac had helped her skating technique as he hoped. She was stronger and fitter and more content than she had been for months. But Zac wasn't here now. And all their training, all the hours of hard work, would be for nothing if he didn't come back.

♥

It was Wednesday, and the show was only three days away. Brock's optimism was faltering. 'You've got to do something,' he told her sharply. 'Make it right, Tania.'

'How?'

Brock exclaimed in annoyance. 'I don't know! You're the one who got us into this, so you get us out! I've left message after message for Zac but he's completely *incommunicado*. I need my pairs programme on Saturday. It's too good a programme to miss out – and besides, the schedule has gone to the printers. It has to happen, Tania. Sort it!'

Her skating bag seemed heavier than usual as Tania slung it over her shoulder and made her way up the stairs to the exit. To the left of the main doors was the trophy cabinet she had proudly shown Zac all those weeks ago. Tania stared blankly at the cups and shields. Her name, written over and over again. But for what? Did she really want to be the best if it meant she had to do it on her own?

Tania leaned her forehead against the glass and thought. *How can I put things right? How can I explain to Zac in such a way that he won't be angry with me any more? What can I do?*

She could buy him a present to say sorry . . .

She could arrange for him to spend another day at SkyJumpers . . .

She could sort out something so that he didn't have to work in the pub all the time . . .

Tania banged her head against the glass. *Stupid, stupid!* They all involved money! And that was the problem, wasn't it? Zac didn't want her money. What *did* he want?

She tilted her head so she could see the reflection of the rink in the glass. Round and round went the skaters. Tracing patterns on the rink . . . Her name on all these trophies . . . How to say sorry . . . Something Libby had said ages ago . . .

A peculiar image started to form in her head. But that kind of thing was impossible, wasn't it? Or . . . maybe not . . .

Chapter 18

only chance to put things right

'You want to do *what*?' asked Caroline in astonishment.

'Go to the rink tomorrow night at midnight,' said Tania.

Caroline looked at her husband. Alistair frowned. 'I don't think so,' he said. 'Not in the middle of the night.'

'What for?' asked Caroline. 'Brock wouldn't ask you to do something like that.'

'No, it's not for Brock.' Tania twisted her fingers together. She knew it was a big ask. 'I can't really explain. But it's important.'

'You need your sleep for the show on Saturday,' Caroline reminded her. 'I don't like you going out only two nights before. And you've got school on Friday morning before the dress rehearsal.'

'Trust me,' said Tania. 'Please. It's important to me.'

'Well . . .' said Caroline.

'The rink will be closed at that time,' objected Alistair.

Tania shook her head. 'No, it won't. I was lucky. The manager said I can have it for half an hour.'

'Half an hour,' said Caroline, bewildered. 'What are you doing for half an hour?'

'I can't tell you. Really, I can't.'

'It's not illegal, is it?' demanded Alistair suddenly.

'No, Dad.' Tania smiled. 'Honestly. It's not dangerous either. It's just – something I want to do. Need to do. I did something wrong, and this is my chance to put it right.'

Caroline put a hand on her husband's arm. 'Let her do it. It's not like she's been untrustworthy before.'

Alistair looked at Tania for a long moment, and then he nodded. 'All right. But at twelve-thirty, we're coming in to fetch you. And we'll be outside in the car the whole time.'

♥

'What are you going to do?' asked Libby.

'I don't want to tell you,' said Tania, 'in case it doesn't work.'

'But it's something to do with skating, right?'

'Yes.' Tania shook her head. 'But that's not why I rang you. I wanted to ask about you and Scott. And the girl in the music shop. You never really told me what happened.'

'Yes I did. He just went straight home. There wasn't anything to tell.' But there was hesitation in Libby's voice.

'What's up? Have you found out something else?' Tania's heart sank for her friend. '*Has* he been cheating on you?'

Libby made an indistinguishable noise that sounded like, 'Uhmm-hummm.'

'Libby, you can tell me.'

'Well . . .' Libby sounded as though she was squirming. 'He wasn't *exactly* cheating, no . . .'

'What do you mean, not exactly?'

'All right, he wasn't at all,' said Libby. 'He did admit he'd been lying to me though, about where he was all the time.'

Tania felt relieved that Scott hadn't let Libby down, but she was puzzled. 'So what was he doing?'

'He was recording me a song.' Libby sounded more and more embarrassed. 'He wrote me a song, and he wanted to get it recorded properly, like professionally. The girl in the shop has a boyfriend who works for a music studio.'

'And she got him a slot.'

'Right. I got the CD today, posted through my letterbox.'

Tania felt something inside her twinge with jealousy. 'That's so romantic, Libby. What's the song like?'

'Oh, well, you know . . . about how much he loves me, all that . . .'

Tania could guess Libby was probably blushing, but she knew her friend would be bursting with pride. 'Aren't you excited?' she asked. 'I mean, wow! He wrote you a *song*! That's amazing!'

'I know,' said Libby. 'It's just that now I feel really guilty about suspecting him. He texted me a minute ago to ask if I'd listened to the CD yet.' She gave a shaky laugh. 'He said, *Now you'll know how I really feel about you.*'

'Wow.'

'And the song is completely *dripping* in romance. Oh, Tania, what am I going to *do*?'

'What do you mean?' asked Tania, amused. 'You've got the perfect boyfriend!'

'I know!' wailed Libby. 'But I'm not used to it! I keep having to pinch myself. After all those useless boys who cheated on me or dumped me after the first date – I finally found one who's worth it.'

'But you really like him too, right?'

'I *adore* him!'

Tania laughed. 'Then there's nothing to worry about, is there?'

'I guess not.' Libby let out a little sigh. 'I'll just have to be blissfully happy for the rest of my life.'

Tania was silent.

'Tan? You still there?'

'Yeah.'

Libby made a sympathetic noise. 'You're thinking about Zac, aren't you? It'll be OK, you'll see. He'll come round. Whatever it is you're doing, I'm sure it will work.'

'I'm not,' said Tania. 'I don't even know if I can pull it off.'

'You just have to promise me,' begged Libby, 'that you'll text me the minute you've done whatever it is. You have to let me know what happens.'

'It'll be the middle of the night,' warned Tania.

'I don't care,' said Libby. 'You and Zac are meant to be together. Just like me and Scott. I just know it.'

♥

Brock wasn't at the rink the next morning, and for once, Tania was grateful. She didn't want him asking a lot of awkward questions. A couple of solo skaters were practising their routines for the show, but otherwise the rink was quiet and she was able to find a small space on the ice to practise.

It was tricky; much trickier than she had imagined. She had to go back and look at her tracings each time, and they weren't anything like as good as she had hoped. After an hour's practice, Tania's legs ached and she was dying for a coffee. A learner class was just coming onto the ice, so she had to take a break anyway.

Tania took off her boots and made her way to the little café by the main entrance. 'Cappuccino, please,' she said.

'Want a choc-chip cookie with that?' asked the girl. 'Special offer price today.'

Tania accepted, and found a small table where she sat down and broke off a piece of the cookie. At the table behind her, a large woman was holding forth to her smaller, glassy-eyed companion. 'Far too expensive, that's what I've told her,' said the woman. 'It's a good hobby, I said, but don't expect to skate professionally. Besides, what kind of a career is it anyway? You get to twenty-five, you're on the shelf. It's a sport for the young, and unless you're right at the top, there's no point even entering. That's what I told my Connie anyway.'

'You're probably right, Meg,' said the other woman.

'I know I am,' replied Meg, taking a large bite of a cheese scone. 'She's good, Connie is. That coach she's got says she could be really good – got natural talent. She could do well. But *how* well?'

The other woman muttered something.

'There's no guarantee of that, is there?' said Meg. 'And what if she doesn't make it? Connie's a sensible girl. I've explained it all to her, and she's coming round to my way of thinking. She loves it, of course – well, they all do when they're little girls, don't they? It's like ballet. They all want the pretty dresses and to dance on their toes. But will she really work hard when she needs to? Hours and hours every week – and you know who'll have to take and fetch her, of course.'

'You will,' said the other woman.

'Exactly! Now, all I want is for my little girl to be happy, but I'd far rather she did something with more prospects. If she puts her whole life into skating, what on earth will she do after that? Much better, I told Connie, to concentrate on her school work. That'll get her into university and a stable job. And she can carry on skating in her spare time. As a hobby.'

'How did she take that?'

'Well,' Meg said, 'she didn't like it, of course. Burst

into tears and said skating was her whole life, it was all she wanted to do, she'd work her fingers to the bone and all that. But in years to come she'll be glad she's got something else to offer.'

'You think she'll forget about it?'

Meg considered. 'Maybe not for a while. And it doesn't help when she sees other skaters around here. Wants to be like that Tania Dunn, she says.'

The other woman sighed. 'Such a lovely skater.'

'Not been doing so well lately though, has she?' asked Meg. 'We've all noticed; everyone who comes to the rink knows she's been failing the jumps. Can't imagine why she's been paired with that boy for the show. They've been doing some fancy footwork, but it won't help her reach the Olympics, will it? I think she's a child star – you know, one of those who shows early promise but never makes it into the big time. I said to Connie, I said, look what happens when you pour your heart and soul into something and it doesn't work out. What's that Tania going to do if she can't skate, eh? Built her up too much, they have. She's got a long way to fall.'

Tania's ears were burning and she felt sick. Was that what people really thought of her? That she was burned out; all washed up? She poked miserably at her cookie and kept her head down. Why did she even care what that Meg woman thought? Was it because secretly, deep down, she was terrified they were right?

But then Tania thought of Zac. He brought out the best in her. It wasn't just about fancy footwork. When she was skating with him, she was better than when she skated on her own, she knew it. And with that certainty came a hot, scorching desire to prove them all wrong. They would see what she could really do. At the Winter Ice Spectacular . . .

But there would be no Ice Show without Zac. Tania's head snapped up. She drained her coffee, stood up, hefted her bag over her shoulder and made her way back to the ice, deliberately catching the eye of the woman called Meg on her way out, whose jaw dropped.

Tania laced up her skates, her lips pressed tight. It was a crazy idea, she knew, but she had to make it work. It was her only chance to put things right.

Chapter 19

i really am sorry

The rink was eerie at night. Outside, it was cloudy, with few stars appearing. Inside, there was minimal lighting, casting a ghostly glow over the ice. Tania gave a slight shiver as she looked down at the luminescent surface. So busy during the day, it was strange to see it empty.

'Funny time for extra practice,' commented Jim, the facilities manager.

'I'm meeting someone here.'

Jim raised his eyebrows. 'Ah, I get it. Late-night romantic skate, is that it?'

'Sort of,' said Tania. She bit her lip. 'If he comes, that is.'

'Course he will,' said Jim. 'If it's you he's meeting.'

Tania smiled. 'Thanks, Jim.'

'Twenty-one years I've worked here,' Jim told her, 'and never seen a prettier skater than you.'

'Well, let's hope you're right,' said Tania, 'otherwise I'll be skating with you instead.'

Jim let out a laugh. 'Not on your life! I work around the rink, not on it. You wouldn't catch me trying a toe loop.'

Tania glanced at the large digital clock on the wall. Ten minutes to midnight. 'I've got to get ready,' she told Jim. She didn't have much time.

At one minute to midnight, Tania was poised on the ice, waiting, her eyes fixed on the doors to the main entrance. Her heart beat so loudly in her ears it seemed to echo around the silent rink. The chill from the ice crept into her boots, but she didn't dare shake her feet to warm them. Jim had disappeared into his office with the promise that he would be back in a few minutes. 'Don't want to cramp your style,' he'd said with a wink.

So now, Tania waited. The digital clock display showed midnight exactly. Tania clenched her fists. *He must come, he must!* She thought back over the last three months. It was almost as though she had been living a different life before she met Zac. She could never have imagined that they would get on. He was a daredevil, wasn't he? Threw himself around with no thought of injury or of perfecting his moves. But then . . . There was the other side of him. The side in which his parents worked night and day to bring in enough money to send him to skating lessons, even though he claimed it was 'just for fun'. The side in which he was studying sciences and maths with an eye on the future. That side of him wasn't reckless at all. That side was dedicated and loyal and thoughtful, and . . .

And I love him, Tania thought suddenly. It was so clear it was almost as though she had spoken it out loud. *I love him. I love him.* For how long had she been in love? Now she had realized, it was as though she had always loved him. No one moment; no single event had made her love him. It was the hours of practice; the conversations over ballet or buying skates. It was the gradual realization that her life was so much better with him in it.

The clock showed two minutes past midnight. *He's not coming*, she thought. *And I can't tell him how I feel. I can't even say sorry.*

An awful choking feeling took hold of her and suddenly it was hard to breathe. *How can I go on*, she thought, *if he doesn't know?*

The main doors banged, and Tania nearly fell over from shock.

Zac walked into the rink, frowning. He looked down at the ice.

Tania looked up at him, and the choking sensation

evaporated entirely. An immense feeling of calm and warmth spread through her. He stood there, the dim light catching the blond spikes of his hair, staring down at the rink. She couldn't see the expression in his eyes from this distance, but she felt as though he were looking right into her soul. She bent down to her right boot and unscrewed the tiny cap on the bottle attached to her ankle. Then, glancing up to make sure he was still there, she began.

An opening sweep in a huge 'S' shape that covered the width of the rink. Then a careful change of edge into a small spin . . . two hockey stops, and a looping move, before a couple of sharp turns, a small spin with a looped tail, and a sweeping curve to finish.

Tania looked back at her tracings. Standing out sharply against the cold blue of the ice, was a trail of red paint, dripped out of the bottle on her ankle. It was wobbly, and the paint had run out just before the end, but the writing was clear:

Sorry Zac.

Hesitantly Tania looked up. Would he still be there?

Not only was Zac there, but he was leaning over the upper barrier, staring at the ice; an expression of delight on his face. 'How did you do that?' he called, his voice ringing across the ice. 'That's brilliant!'

Tania felt weak with relief. 'Paint bottle on my ankle,' she called back, lifting her foot to show him.

'Stay there,' he said. 'I'm coming down.'

Tania skated over to the barrier to meet him, her stomach suddenly full of butterflies.

'Show me,' said Zac as he reached the bottom of the stairs. 'How did you attach it and make sure it came out so smoothly?'

Tania unlaced her boot and passed it over. 'I had to thin it down,' she said. 'I wanted to use ink but I thought it would stain the ice too badly.'

'Yeah, you'd never get that out,' said Zac, grinning. 'Can you imagine Brock's face tomorrow if he found that written into the ice just a day before his precious show?'

'He'd never forgive me,' said Tania.

'Too right,' said Zac. 'But this is brilliant. A paint bottle. And you just stuck it on at the right angle?'

'I wasn't even sure it would work,' confessed Tania. 'I didn't have a chance to practise with the paint at all.'

'But you must have spent hours working on the tracings,' said Zac, glancing back at the ice. 'To make sure you did all of that on the right foot.'

'I've been practising all day.'

Zac raised his eyebrows. 'All *day*?'

'Yeah. When I could get on the ice, that is.'

Zac said nothing.

'I wanted to make sure I got it right,' Tania went on, the words starting to rush out of her. 'I wanted to say sorry, but not just – you know. But I thought – on the ice. Well, it's more – personal, sort of. Because I really am sorry – I felt so awful about everything. I should have told you – asked you. I didn't think about what you would – how you'd feel.' She stopped, her face bright red.

Zac looked serious for a moment. He nodded slowly. 'I've been doing some thinking too,' he said. 'I know you didn't realize what it meant. You've always had money – I haven't.'

'I know, and that's why—'

Zac held up a hand. 'Let me finish. Brock's been leaving me phone messages all week. Telling me I have responsibilities, trying to guilt-trip me. But he also talked about you.' He stared out across the ice. 'He said I shouldn't be too hard on you, because having money could be a disadvantage in some ways. It makes people think that everything can be solved with money, whereas if you don't have it, you know that there are other things just as important. Like family, respect – trust.' He looked directly at Tania. 'I trusted you. I trusted you to be honest with me. But I can see how you wanted to help. You thought I'd be offended if you just gave me the money.'

'Wouldn't you?' Tania couldn't help saying.

'Yes, probably,' said Zac. 'But you never gave me the chance to give my opinion. You lied to me.'

'I know.'

'You were wrong.'

'I know that too. I'm so sorry.' Tania took another shaky breath. 'Thank you for coming.'

'Yeah, well, you got me. Always wanted to know what this place was like with no one here. And your note was kind of cryptic.' He looked at the red writing on the ice again, and a smile spread across his face. 'It was worth it. This is one of the coolest things I've seen. However did you think of it?'

'The names on the trophies in the cabinet,' said Tania, biting her lip. 'It was the reflection of the ice in the glass. And the names.'

Zac nodded. 'So you thought about writing on the ice with your blades. Brilliant.'

Tania shifted from one foot to the other. 'So,' she said in a small voice, 'are you – do you forgive me?'

Zac looked at her. Meeting his gaze, those hazel eyes, was too much for Tania. She had to look away, frightened of what he might say. 'Hey,' said Zac, and his voice was soft. 'How could I be angry with you, after this? It took real guts to think this up and see it through. In the middle of the night too.'

'It was the only time the rink was empty,' whispered Tania.

'You're lucky no one saw it,' said Zac. He chuckled. 'Jim would have a fit.'

Tania's eyes opened wide. 'He's in his office! He said he'd be back in a few minutes! I've got to clean it off!'

Zac burst out laughing. 'What are you like! Is this the same Tania Dunn who was obsessed with perfecting the double axel and who wouldn't take risks on the ice?'

'Don't laugh,' pleaded Tania. 'I've really got to clean it all off.'

'Don't worry,' said Zac. He grinned. 'I'll help you. Besides . . .'

She looked up at him. 'What?'

A funny look came into Zac's eyes. 'I can't skate a pairs programme on graffiti.'

Tania swallowed. 'Really?'

He nodded, staring at her. 'Can't let my partner down, can I? Only thing is, I don't seem to have any skates. Think I must have left mine somewhere.'

Tania's face broke into a huge smile. 'That's lucky,' she said, 'because I happen to have a pair in your size that are all ready to wear.' She pointed to Zac's skates, which were sitting neatly on a bench.

'That's lucky then,' said Zac, and smiled.

Chapter 20

more than anything

The audience clapped appreciatively as the group of novice skaters took their bows. Dressed in costumes from *Alice in Wonderland*, their programme had gone down a storm. The rink side was packed with family and friends and those who just liked skating, as well as coaches and agents from farther afield, who had come with an eye out for the next Sasha Cohen or Torvill and Dean.

Behind a curtain that shaded the skaters from the audience, Tania and Zac waited. There was one more programme to go before their turn.

'You look great,' Zac murmured.

Tania flushed. She had worn the catsuit the day before, for the dress rehearsal, but she still hadn't quite got used to it. It was so very revealing; she felt almost naked. Not helped, of course, by Zac's gaze, which had swept over her from head to toe before he whistled appreciatively. At that moment, she had almost blurted it all out – how she felt about him; her terror that they would never skate together again – everything. But she had bitten back the words. She had only just won him back. She couldn't afford to frighten him off so soon, especially just before the show.

Today, Tania had taken pains with her appearance. As well as the catsuit with its swirling blue whirlpool of sequins, she had added silver and blue sparkles to the side of her face and her hair. She had even painted her nails silver to complete the look. Zac had been quite dazzled when he saw the final effect. 'I didn't realize your eyes were so blue,' he eventually managed.

The little girl waiting nervously beside them took a deep breath and prepared to step onto the ice. 'Good luck, Connie,' said her coach, and Tania blinked with recognition at the name. Connie looked about nine years old and was wearing a baby-pink skating dress, with a tiny tiara perched on top of her head. For a moment, Tania forgot her own nerves as she watched Connie take up position on the ice. The music began, and the little girl started to skate. Tania's eyes opened wide: this girl was very good indeed.

'She looks like a mini-you,' whispered Zac, his gaze also following what little they could see of Connie through the gap in the curtain.

'She's better than I was,' said Tania. An anger was rising in her against the woman called Meg who thought skating wasn't as important as a stable career. She said fiercely. 'She's as good as Kerri was.'

Zac nodded. 'She should go far.'

'I'll tell her that. Someone should look out for her.'

Zac looked a little surprised but didn't comment. Instead, he peered out of the gap in the curtain. 'My parents are here,' he suddenly said. 'Wow! I didn't think they'd come.'

'Where?' Tania squeezed up close so she could see out too.

Zac pointed. 'There. Sitting by the aisle. My mum's got long brown hair like you. Dad's next to her in the blue jacket.'

'They took the afternoon off to come and see the show,' said Tania.

'A Saturday too,' said Zac, sounding as though he couldn't quite believe it. 'They *never* take time off together.' His face split into a smile.

'They must really want to see you skate,' said Tania.

Zac glanced down. Their faces were only inches away. 'I guess,' he said, and his voice was husky.

Tania gazed into his face – the one she had come to love. 'Zac . . .' she said.

'I know,' said Zac.

'You do?' Tania's heart skipped a beat.

'Yeah.' His hand found Tania's and he squeezed it. 'Can't believe this is the last time we'll skate together,' he said quietly.

Tania gulped. *That's not what I was going to say*, she thought.

'Not sure I want to go back to skating on my own,' said Zac, with a half-laugh.

Tania stared out at Connie, unseeing. 'Then don't,' she whispered.

'What?' Zac bent to hear her. 'What did you say?'

She looked up at him. 'Don't. Don't go back to skating on your own. Skate with me.'

They stared at each other. 'Are you . . .' began Zac.

There was a sudden burst of applause. Connie's programme had finished.

'It's our turn,' said Tania.

Zac nodded, his eyes never leaving hers. 'You ready?'

Tania breathed in. Excitement and impatience surged through her. A huge smile spread across her face. 'Yes.'

He answered her smile with his own. 'Then let's go.'

Connie, her cheeks flushed to match her pink dress, stepped off the ice. Tania grabbed her arm as she passed. 'Don't let them stop you,' she said firmly. 'If you want to skate, don't let anyone tell you you can't.'

Connie stared at her. 'I won't,' she said solemnly. 'Thank you, Tania.'

Tania nodded, then Zac was pulling her onto the ice and into position.

She barely heard the applause as they took up the opening pose. Her whole attention was focused on Zac. The music started, and Tania felt her body respond by itself. By now, every move was so familiar to her that she gave herself up to the ice.

They moved in perfect harmony. Instinctively Zac reached for Tania at precisely the right moments. The air whistled past them as they built up speed around the end of the rink before Tania held out a boot for Zac to grab and lift her into a stag position. There was cheering, but Tania was oblivious. Adrenalin fizzed through her like a firework, and by the look on Zac's face, she could tell he felt the same. They exchanged looks of pure delight, and the death spiral was the best they had ever done it.

The programme started conventionally enough, but before too long they were into Zac's skateboarding section. There were gasps from the crowd as Zac used his knees to skid across the ice, and Tania performed two cartwheels in succession. Then the audience burst into spontaneous applause. Tania felt her body flood with excitement, and it felt just like the moment on the zip-wire, when she launched herself into space.

As they went into a pairs spin, Tania was acutely aware of Zac's hands on her, as though they were burning through her costume. The spin increased speed, and for a moment it was hard to tell where Tania ended and Zac began.

The music built to a climax and Tania felt her heart beat faster. This was it – the tabletop lift. Without hesitation, she sprang up, and Zac lifted her high above his head, his blades skimming the ice below her. Tania closed her eyes for a second, arms stretched out. This was true joy – this was flying.

As though she were a delicate piece of china, Zac lowered her swiftly into their fish dive, and as the music came to an end, Tania turned her head to look back into his eyes. The expression in his matched how she was feeling – more alive than she had ever felt before. Her hand brushed his cheek, tracing the outline of his jaw without thinking. Zac's lips moved.

'You know I'm crazy about you, don't you?' he was saying. His words were drowned out by the crowd, but Tania knew she had heard him right. She couldn't reply; the breath stopped in her lungs. She felt dizzy at the look in his eyes. It was as though she were at the centre of his world and nothing else existed.

He set her on her feet, and suddenly Tania was aware of the audience. They were on their feet, clapping and cheering, and as Tania looked out, she caught sight of her parents, standing and cheering with the rest of them. Beside them were Libby and Scott. Libby was whooping so loudly Tania could hear her over everyone else.

Zac said out of the corner of his mouth, 'I think we're meant to bow.'

Tania blinked. 'Of course.'

They bowed to all four sides of the rink. The applause just grew louder and louder, and to her satisfaction, Tania caught a glimpse of Connie's mother Meg, on her feet and clapping just as enthusiastically as everyone else.

It was time to leave the ice, but for one moment, Tania paused. Her eyes slid across the audience, drinking it all in. *This is what I love*, she told herself. *This is what I lost. But now I've found it again*.

They skated to the side, where around seventy skaters were waiting to come on for the big finale. Brock nodded to them as he corralled the smaller ones together. It was a nod of approval, and although he didn't say anything, they knew he was pleased. Tania and Zac moved to the back as the others poured past them, and then, suddenly, they were alone.

'I guess we should get changed,' said Tania.

Zac reached for her hand. 'Wait a minute,' he said. 'Before – when we were waiting to skate. You said – did you mean it? Do you want us to keep skating as a pair?'

Tania looked into his eyes, and her gaze didn't falter. 'More than anything,' she told him.

Zac opened his mouth to speak, but his breath caught in his throat. 'I was hoping you'd say that,' he whispered. 'I can't imagine coming here every day and not skating with you.' He grinned. 'I guess we should get changed then, like you said.'

'One thing first,' said Tania, as he turned to go. 'Out there, on the ice. What did you say?'

He looked steadily at her. 'You heard me.'

'I want you to say it again.'

Zac glanced down and reached for her other hand. He held them out in front of him. 'I said I'm crazy about you.'

Tania couldn't speak, she felt so happy.

'Didn't you know?' asked Zac. 'I thought it must be obvious how I felt about you.'

She shook her head.

'Every day, when I wake up,' he told her, 'you're the first thing I think about. Seeing you – skating with you. You make my day better – you make my life better.'

Tania eyes shone. 'That's how I feel too,' she whispered.

Beyond the curtain, far away, the crowd erupted into applause.

'Then I guess there's just one thing left to do,' said Zac softly. He reached for her face, and slowly, as the cheers grew louder, he bent his head to hers and kissed her.

♥

You can meet some of the Sweet Hearts girls again
in the fantastic new book

Model
Behaviour

Available soon

Read on to find out who . . .

'You're with the dogs today,' Dan told them. 'Ian's in charge there but if you don't see him, Harry will show you what to do. You'll need to take the dogs out for their daily walk – he'll go with you the first time.'

Lola twisted her fingers together. Although Harry had been surprisingly good company the day before, she wasn't anxious to see him again, not after he'd been so rude about her dream job.

There was a knock at the door. 'Come in!' called Dan.

The door opened, and a stylishly dressed woman with a friendly expression looked in. 'Oh, sorry, I didn't realize you were in the middle of something.'

'It's fine. Mrs Dunn, isn't it? You've come to pick up Sheba.'

'That's right.' A pretty dark-haired girl appeared next to the woman. 'Is she ready?'

Dan smiled. 'Raring to go. I'll just need your mum to sign some paperwork. Do you want to go and pick up Sheba yourself, Tania?'

Her expression brightened. 'Can I?'

'Of course. Lola and Naiha will take you.' Dan turned to them. 'Sheba is the border collie. Far left – Ian or Harry will show you. In fact, get Harry to open the pen for you since he knows Sheba.'

Lola nodded. She and Naiha led Tania round the

side of the office and towards the dog pens. 'Tania?' asked Naiha, her brow furrowed. 'Did you say your name was Tania Dunn?'

'Yes, that's right.' The dark-haired girl looked curious. 'Why?'

'Are you an ice skater? Sorry, I know that's a bit of a random question.'

Lola's eyebrows rose. Of course! They'd been to the Winter Ice Spectacular just before Christmas. Tania had done an amazing routine with her partner.

Tania went pink. 'Yes, that's me.'

'We saw you skate,' Lola told her. 'At Christmas.'

'You were *amazing*!' added Naiha.

'Thanks.' Tania looked pleased. 'It went better than we'd thought it would.'

'I'd never have dared do all that stuff,' Naiha went on. 'Didn't he lift you over his head at one point?'

Tania grinned. 'Yes. I was a bit terrified by that one.'

'You didn't look it,' Lola said.

'Well, I have a good partner. I knew he wouldn't let me fall.'

Naiha glanced around before saying, 'Are you and him – I mean . . .'

Tania coughed. 'Uh, yeah. Yeah, we are.'

'He is *hot*,' Naiha said, nodding for emphasis.

Tania gave a laugh. 'You sound just like my friend Libby.'

'Well, he is!'

'Thanks – I think so too.' Tania went even pinker.

Lola was rather sorry they'd arrived at the dog pens; Tania was practically a celebrity in Parchester. A sudden thought struck her, and she reached out to stop Tania going in. 'I don't suppose you ever go to the Kellerman club, do you?'

'Why?'

'My stepfather runs it,' Lola said, wondering if this was going to get her into trouble. 'They're doing a massive makeover soon and they're going to do floor-to-ceiling posters. They need people to be photographed doing gym stuff.'

'Really? You never told me!' exclaimed Naiha.

'I was going to,' said Lola. Naiha snorted. 'But I wondered – do you think you'd be up for doing a shoot? I mean, you can't skate there, but you do ballet and other stuff, don't you? And you're a – a kind of local celebrity.' *It would be a massive scoop for the club! And maybe Tania and I could be in a shot together, doing yoga or something really cool . . . people know who she is, I'd be working with someone famous!*

Tania looked interested. 'I don't know. I mean, yeah, it sounds kind of fun. Hang on . . .' She reached into

her bag. 'Let me give you my number. You can pass it
on if you like.' She scribbled on a piece of scrap paper.
'There you go.'

'Thanks!' Lola ignored the glowering stare her
friend was giving her. Harry had just appeared in a
further part of the yard and she called over to him.
'Hi, Harry! Tania's come to pick up Sheba.'

Harry looked up and Lola was conscious of a
feeling of surprise. Had he *brushed his hair*? There
was something a bit different about it – was that *gel*
in it? 'OK,' he said. 'I'll get her.'

Naiha sighed. 'Everyone's fixed up except me.'

'What do you mean?' Tania asked.

'You've got your gorgeous partner . . .'

'Zac.'

'Yeah. And Lola's got Samir, though she doesn't
appreciate him.'

'Hey!'

'And who have I got?' Naiha thrust out an arm dramatically. A dog shot out of a pen and leaped up at
her, wagging its tail furiously and barking. 'Argh! Get
off!'

'Sheba!' cried Tania. The dog immediately turned to
her, barking with delight. Tania bent down to stroke
her, grinning. 'Hello, darling, we've come to take you
home with us.'